THE MINER'S MOLL

"Quiet, girl!" Spur said. "We're here to help you."

He holstered his weapon and quietly ran down the stairs.

"Come on!" McCoy yelled to Kincaid and the girl.

The three of them hurried down the stairs. Spur surveyed the scene as they descended into the saloon.

"Hey!" a lean cowboy shouted, staring at the trio. "They're taking away the new girl!"

Spur crashed through two sodden men. He and Kincaid rushed toward the door, fighting through the angry drunks bent on keeping the new girl at their disposal.

Suddenly, Spur saw a knife slicing through the air toward them.

Also in the *Spur* Series:

SPUR #1: ROCKY MOUNTAIN VAMP

SPUR #2: CATHOUSE KITTEN

SPUR #3: INDIAN MAID

SPUR #4: SAN FRANCISCO STRUMPET

SPUR #5: WYOMING WENCH

SPUR #6: TEXAS TART

SPUR #7: MONTANA MINX

SPUR #8: SANTA FE FLOOZY

SPUR #9: SALT LAKE LADY

SPUR #10: NEVADA HUSSY

SPUR #11: NEBRASKA NYMPH

SPUR #12: GOLD TRAIN TRAMP

SPUR #13: RED ROCK REDHEAD

SPUR #14: SAVAGE SISTERS

SPUR #15: HANG SPUR McCOY!

SPUR #16: RAWHIDER'S WOMAN

SPUR #17: SALOON GIRL

SPUR #18: MISSOURI MADAM

SPUR #19: HELENA HELLION

SPUR #20: COLORADO CUTIE

SPUR #21: TEXAS TEASE

SPUR #22: DAKOTA DOXY

SPUR #23: SAN DIEGO SIRENS

SPUR #24: DODGE CITY DOLL

SPUR #25: LARAMIE LOVERS

SPUR #26: BODIE BEAUTIES

SPUR #27: FRISCO FOXES

SPUR #28: KANSAS CITY CHORINE

SPUR #29: PLAINS PARAMOUR

SPUR #30: BOISE BELLE

SPUR #31: PORTLAND PUSSYCAT

SPUR #32

THE MINER'S MOLL

DIRK FLETCHER

LEISURE BOOKS NEW YORK CITY

A LEISURE BOOK®

January 2006

Published by

Dorchester Publishing Co., Inc.
200 Madison Avenue
New York, NY 10016

ISBN 0-8439-2992-8

The name "Leisure Books" and the stylized "L" with design are
trademarks of Dorchester Publishing Co., Inc.

Printed in the United States of America.

Visit us on the web at www.dorchesterpub.com.

THE MINER'S MOLL

CHAPTER ONE

Carl Mond knelt behind the rain barrel. He heard Jedidiah's scuffling feet next to him but didn't take the time to glance at his partner. The streets were deserted. All good folk had been in bed for hours. Even Ma's saloon—The Motherlode—was silent.

Oreville, Nevada, slept under a silvery, crescent moon.

"Carl."

Mond waved him off.

"Carl!" The voice was louder. Too loud.

"Quiet. What the hell is it?" Mond whispered as the cool desert air swept around them, driving stinging particles of sand into his eyes. He rubbed them out and continued surveying the street.

"Mebbe we—"

Carl sighed at the tremor in Jed's voice. "You ain't turnin' yellow on me, is you Steele?"

"But hell! Don't you want yer hundred bucks? It'd

take you months to prop'rly earn that much! Quit yer bellyachin'. We got a job to do."

Mond turned, catching Steele staring at the ground. He grabbed the man's shoulder. "Right?"

"Okey. Okey, Carl! It just feels bad."

The two men crept along the street and halted at the corner of Woody's Dry Goods.

The street was still clear. Their destination was just across the street. Mond snapped his head in both directions. No one moved down Main.

Energy surged through him. Carl tapped Jed's shoulder. As they hurried across the broad, dusty avenue, Mond retrieved the three skeleton keys from his coat pocket. They softly jangled. He muffled the cold steel with his fingers and pushed on.

Rattle. Hooves clomping into the dirt. Leather twitching.

A carriage.

Mond grabbed Jed's plaid shirt and yanked him from their target into the gloom surrounding the assayer's office. They melted into the shadows and waited.

Jed Steele's breath was so loud Mond thought the men could hear it at the silver mine across the desert. He clapped a hand over his partner's mouth and froze as the one-horse carriage clunked by them. The sound of its passing died out.

"Dang near choked me!" Jed said as Carl removed his hand.

"Better than being seen." He wiped his palm on his knee. "That carriage must've turned onto Main from Parker. Come on. We got work to do!"

After a quick look, they ran to the small, wooden

structure. The front porch squeaked as Mond slipped the first skeleton into the lock. It wouldn't budge.

Wouldn't you know it, he thought, trying the second one. Another breeze sent the smell of Jed's fear into the air. Carl Mond cursed and yanked out the useless second key.

"Come on!" Jed whispered into his ear.

"Shut up!"

Carl's hands were chilled. The small ring slipped from his fingers and crashed onto the porch. His face flushed as he picked it up and studied the keys in the thin moonlight.

Which ones had he tried? Which ones wouldn't work? No time for thinking. Mond slid a likely key into the lock and tried to turn it.

To the left, no go.

To the right, a slight hesitation. Then success.

Mond smiled and pressed against the knob. The two men hustled inside and quietly closed the door.

The dim light that shone through the windows made everything inside the building a dull grey.

"Whew!" Jed said. "When you dropped the keys I—"

"Shut up. This thing ain't over yet!" He stuck out his chin. "Draw yer weapon, Jed. Eyeball outside the winders. We were on that damned porch for too long. Someone might'a seen us."

"Okay."

Carl Mond leaped over the long, waist-high counter, amazed at how easy this had been so far. Just like they'd been told. He stared back at the barely visible wooden boxes, stacks of U.S. stamps, receipts, pens and bottles of inks that littered the counter.

He never figured it'd be this easy to break into the post office.

Carl frowned and stood before the left door behind the counter. That was the one he wanted. That was the one he'd been told to go into.

The first skeleton key easily turned the lock. He pulled on the knob and went inside.

It was a small, black room. Unable to see but unwilling to strike a light, Carl Mond kicked through the darkness, searching for his prize. His boot banged into two soft objects and sent them sliding away.

The heavy one, he remembered. Take the heavy one.

He plunged a hand into the void. Carl's fingers raced along the dusty floorboards. He felt a smooth, polished object and gripped it. Too narrow, he thought.

Then it moved.

"Sheeit!" Mond stormed from the storage room and threw the creature. It sailed across the counter and landed at Jedidiah Steele's feet. The snake slithered away.

"Hurry up!" Jed said, stepping back from the window. "You was the one in the rush and you're playing with snakes. Find it yet?"

"Shut up!"

Carl grimaced and returned to the closet. He found the two sacks, weighed them in his hands and chose the undeniably heavier one. He hauled it from the small room.

Jed went to the counter. "You shore that's the

right bag? I don't wanna come back here again."

"Yeah." He climbed over the counter. "Let's go."

The canvas bag was so heavy that Carl Mond had to sling it over his shoulder. He gripped Steele's arm as the man stretched his hand to the doorknob.

"Check outside first, damnit!"

"Oh, right."

Carl leaned over Jed's shoulder as Steele cracked open the door.

"Don't see nothing."

"Then let's git!" he whispered back.

Steele pushed the door fully open.

The elderly Chinese man stared up at them in surprise from where he crouched on the porch. Jed Steele cursed. Mond dropped the sack, drew and fired a slug into the man's heart. He'd already retrieved the mail sack as the Chinese groaned and flopped onto the boardwalk. His pigtail flipped across his face.

"Run!" Mond yelled as the explosion echoed around the buildings.

They stormed down the alley beside the assayer's office. Doors banged open behind them. Mond put everything he had into his run and urged on Steele who was somewhere behind him.

The heavy canvas bag slammed into his shoulder, carving a dent into the muscled skin.

"Damn!" he said under his breath.

Mond's boots kicked up clouds of dust. He cleared the last ten feet and meshed himself in the thicket of cottonwoods that choked the Merrone River.

"Mond!"

"Right here."

Steele crashed over to him.

"Stop!" he said.

They listened. The whole town was rising. Light bloomed in scattered windows. Men ran past the alleyways through the distant buildings in their nightclothes. A woman screamed.

"Okeh, Steele, we've gotta make the delivery."

"What?" Jed shook his head. "I ain't never moving from here. Never!"

"What you gonna do, swim?" He snorted. "Come on!"

The two men tramped through the saplings and underbrush as Oreville discovered the Chinese man's body and the Merrone River covered the sounds of their movement.

"I don't like it." Julie Golden shook her head and stared at her reflection in the cracked mirror. "Hear me? I don't like it!"

The middleaged, lean man smirked as he pushed the Stetson onto his head. "Too late for your womanly concern, Julie. I'll be back in the morning, and you'd better have it."

She turned to him, crinolines rustling. "Just a minute, Lionel Kemp!" The raven-haired young woman stormed up at him. "You think I'll do anything you say?"

He nodded. "If you wanna keep your pretty little head out of jail."

Julie stepped back at his words, fixing her green eyes on his. "You don't own me."

"I do now. Don't you forget it, woman!"

"But—"

"Shut up, Julie. Open the door for me!"

She took a breath, ran a hand through her hair and sighed. "Open it yourself. I got better things to do."

Lionel Kemp laughed. "You sure are pretty when you're mad. If you didn't have company arriving, I just might—"

"Get out. Get out!" Julie grabbed the silver hairbrush from her table and flung it at the man.

"Careful. You know what'll happen if I get bored with you?"

She sank into the chair in front of the mirror and sighed. "I know what you say you'll do. You don't have any proof. Besides, I didn't do it and no one would believe you."

"So you say. I know better. Keep your skirts clean, Julie. See you in the morning." He looked at the ceiling. "Bacon and eggs sound fine."

"You bastard!"

Lionel Kemp laughed as he walked out of her bedroom.

When he was gone, Julie wiped her eyes. How had she gotten herself into this situation? It was so absurd. But it had happened.

She sat and fiddled with her perfume bottles until the knocking on her door brought her back to reality.

Julie quickly checked her appearance—old habit, she thought with a wry smile—and went downstairs.

The knocking from the kitchen hadn't let up and was so incessant, so loud, that she was infuriated when she opened the door.

"Come in!" she snarled.

Carl Mond and Jedidiah Steele pushed past her.

Their clothing was torn and leaves poked out of their pockets, but Julie ignored that and stared at the canvas bag in Carl's hands.

"Is that it?"

Carl shrugged. "Don't know. Didn't have time to check it."

"We had some trouble," Jed added.

Julie shook her head. "Never mind about that now." She ushered them into the kitchen and checked the heavy, floral draperies that completely covered the windows. They wouldn't be seen.

"What kinda trouble?" Julie asked as Carl laid the bag onto the oak table. "Hell! How we gonna get this thing open?" She flipped the small padlock that secured the top of the canvas bag.

Carl produced the skeleton keys and soon tore the padlock from the grommeted holes.

Despite her anger at Lionel, Julie couldn't resist the urge to see her booty. Maybe he was right. Maybe all women are born criminals.

She reached for the bag and tried to lift it, but a life spent on her back hadn't toughened her arms. "Dump it out on the table!" she said to Carl.

The man upended the mail bag.

Cards and letters spilled from it. A series of small, well-packaged parcels slammed onto the wood. Carl shook it twice to make sure it was empty and threw the canvas sack onto the ground.

Julie ripped open the closest parcel. She tore away the paper and unwrapped the cloth. Ten dazzlingly bright ingots of pure silver poured out from it.

She caught her breath. "You did it." Her excitement died as the men revealed the rest of the silver.

"What was this about trouble?"

"Had to kill a man," Steele said. "Actually, Mond here killed him."

Julie stared at the two. Her face reddened. "Well? Who was it? Who'd you plug?"

"Chin Wah," Mond said, fiddling with the precious metal. "Ran into him right outside the post office. Nothing else to do. He saw our faces."

Julie ignored the surge of emotion. She nodded. "Okay. Don't talk about it."

Mond glanced at Steele. "You aren't, ah, too happy about that?"

She shook her head. "No." Lionel's words bounced around in her head. Julie straightened her back. "No! Of course not! What should have been a clean little robbery's gotten so complicated. Honestly!"

"Didn't you hear the commotion outside? The whole town's up in arms, lookin' for us."

Julie sighed. "I was, ah, busy."

"You got yer silver," Mond said, banging his hand onto the table. "When're we gonna get our money?"

"Right now. Just like I promised you."

Jedidiah Steele rubbed his hands together and licked his lips. Julie sighed and walked to the salt-ware crock where she kept her egg and butter money. She reached into the jar but hesitated.

Did she really trust these men?

A faint scraping sound behind her convinced Julie not to take foolish chances. She slipped the folding money into her hand.

"We'll just take this here silver and be on our way, miss," Carl said.

Julie also grabbed the small, cold object she'd

hidden in the crock and spun to face them. "Sorry, boys. We agreed on a hundred each. Take it or leave it!"

Carl and Jed stared at the deadly little pistol, their mouths open. Each had one hand at his holster, the other on the silver.

"Surprised? You shouldn't be. Just because I'm a woman doesn't mean I'm stupid! Stand back, boys."

They did as they were told.

"Very good!" Smiling, Julie threw the bills onto the table.

Mond and Steele exchanged glances.

"Well? You taking or you leaving? I don't have all night, boys!"

Carl laughed. "Heck, didn't mean nothing by that. Just, ah—ah—" He looked at Steele for help.

"Ah—"

"Testing me?" Julie brightly suggested. "A feeble attempt to see if I have what it takes?"

Mond brightened. "That's it. Just testing you."

"Then I passed. Take the money and get out there. Mix with the crowd that's assuredly gathering, eager to be in on the excitement. I'll be in touch, but stop in the Motherlode Saloon every day to see if I've got more work for you. Gentlemen, I have the feeling this is the start of a beautiful relationship. Just behave yourselves."

"It's beautiful, alright," Carl said as he grabbed his share of the money. "So're you."

"Yeah!" Jed picked up his cash.

Julie smirked. "I'm surprised at you, Carl Mond! This is strictly business. Besides, you can have all you want from my girls at the Motherlode—on the house, like I told you. What would you want with an old woman of thirty? Now git your behinds outa my kitchen!"

"Yes, ma'am." Carl stared down at the money in his hand, folded it and carefully stuffed it into his coat pocket. "We're going."

Julie watched the men walk toward the door. "You sure that Chinese man's really dead?"

"I guess so. We didn't wait to find out," Carl said with a grimace.

The door banged shut behind them.

Alone again, Julie looked at the silver that was scattered across the table top. She laid the derringer in the middle of it; rubbed her eyes and yawned.

It had started. She'd done what the man had told her to do. They had that mine owner's silver. She was safe from Lionel Kemp for another night.

But they'd killed that man . . . .

Julie fought off the revulsion and the tears that threatened her eyes. She locked the kitchen door, gathered up the silver and hid it in the bottom of her pie safe. No one would think to look there, she told herself.

Her work finished, she turned down the kerosene lamps plunging the kitchen into darkness. Julie Golden walked through her silent house, her bootheels clicking on the wooden planks beneath her.

She stifled a yawn, stretched and went to her bedroom.

She never realized she'd lose so much sleep being a criminal.

CHAPTER TWO

He'd seen more Godforsaken towns, but the tiny speck on the map that turned out to be Oreville, Nevada, seemed to be barely alive. Spur McCoy dislodged himself from the stage, collected his carpetbag and stood on the well-packed dirt.

Heat shimmered from the ground and pounded onto him from above, but the air wasn't still. It twisted and banked all around him, sluicing off the nearby mountains like hell-driven demons.

Didn't it ever rain here?

It was a desert town, alright. The buildings hadn't been painted so every wooden plank was the color of dust. The windows at the post office—where the stagecoach's driver was handing over the mailbags—were caked with dirt. Men walking past were similarly coated.

A wind picked up and deposited a pound of dirt on Spur McCoy's face. The howl of millions of particles of sand scraping against each other in the dust devil only increased his dislike of the place. As he brushed off his coat and face, Spur wasn't happy to be in a dying mining town.

But it was his latest assignment as an agent of the Secret Service. Wiping the grit from his eyes, he looked at the two armed men who carefully watched the transfer of mail from the stagecoach. Just as his superior's telegram had informed him, Oreville was in trouble.

Spur got a room at the Eastern Heights Hotel, dropped off his bag and emptied the ewer into the basin. The sound alone refreshed him. He vigorously scrubbed his face. The cool water felt so good after his long stagecoach ride that McCoy finally started to feel good about this case.

He ambled down the street looking for a barber. He had to get some of his hair chopped off in this heat. Spur tried hard to ignore the strength-sapping temperature.

From the looks of things, Oreville must have had a wild past. Money had poured into the place. He saw three assayer's offices, five old dry goods stores, the remains of half a dozen livery stables.

Of the twelve saloons lining Main Street, all but two were abandoned. Their once proud walls sagged. Windows and doors had been ripped from them to furnish new buildings. Three had been burned into huge piles of blackened rubble.

Spur McCoy glanced at the distant mountains. He knew there were mines out there. Gold and silver had brought men to Oreville. A year ago the rich veins had been worked out. Most of the town's men had left, taking their wives and children to more

promising hunting grounds. The only thing keeping
Oreville alive was the last operational silver mine
run by one Cleve P. Magnus.

Spur finally found the familiar red and white pole
and walked into the barbershop.

"Blair's my name; hair's my game," the balding
man said by rote. "Cut or shave?" His round face
carried tired eyes. The barber stropped a razor.

"Uh, just a cut. My hair, I mean."

The barber smiled. "No miner surgery today?"
He whisked the blade back and forth. "I'm
Oreville's doctor, too."

"No. No thanks."

Blair frowned. "Sure. Think you can come in here
and order me around!"

"Look." Spur fit his tall form into the chair. "I
just got into town. Chop off some of my hair, or isn't
my money good enough for you?"

The barber sighed and threw the razor onto the
floor, where it sent a skinny dog yelping and
scurrying out the door. "Sorry, fella. It's been
tough. No work." He fondly smiled. "Used to be
men lined up to get looking good·for their ladies."

"Mine closings?"

"Yep." He grabbed a pair of scissors. "All my
customers left town, and I'm gonna follow them.
I'm gonna be on that stage one day. Never come
back here again."

"Sorry to hear that." Spur removed his hat and
placed it protectively on his chest.

"Yeah, sure." The barber laughed and fastened
a towel around Spur's neck. "But hell, that's my
problem. What's yours?"

"Nothing I can think of." He closed his eyes and

relaxed in the chair.

"If you're here, brother, you got a problem." Blair the barber chuckled and started clipping. "You in town long?"

"Maybe. Don't know."

"Hmm." Clip. Snip. "What you here for?"

"This and that."

"Hm. I'll bet you're one of those men who heard there's still gold hiding like a rattler out there in the mountains, waiting for the man with the right kind of luck to stumble onto it."

"Nope."

"Mmm."

The scissors clacked together. Reddish-brown hair rained around Spur's face.

"You always talk this much?" the barber asked.

McCoy grinned. "Yep."

"Let me give you a piece of advice—no charge," the barber said. "You'll probably want to be seeing the ladies here. Just stay away from Ma's place."

"Ma's?"

"Yeah."

Bored, Spur took the bait. "What's wrong with Ma's place?"

"She has the ugliest girls, the lumpiest beds and the highest prices."

Spur grunted. "Yeah? Then why in hell would anyone go there?"

The barber guffawed. "Shit, man, they got live shows. You know?"

Spur opened his eyes. "Huh?"

Blair's face lit up with steamy memories. "Live shows. You know, girls doing things to each other."

He made a face in the mirror. "Oh."

"Dirty things. Hoo-whee! I just go there for the shows myself—'travagances,' they're called." The bartender grabbed a fat hunk of hair. "You want all this off?"

"No. Don't scalp me! Just take off a little all the way around."

"Why didn't you say so? Jeez! I ain't no mentalist!"

"Just a barber and surgeon."

"Yep. And the town's doctor. You need to get a bullet dug outa your shoulder, you just come to me. Also the undertaker and the notary public."

The barber clipped in silence for a few more minutes.

"Done!" he said, and removed the towel.

Spur glanced in the mirror. He'd had worse haircuts. McCoy flipped a quarter to the man.

"You sure you don't want a shave? I could spruce up those mutton-chop sideburns of yours." Blair retrieved the dirty razor from the corner and held it toward Spur's face. His hand shook from side to side.

"I don't think so. Thanks."

"Right. And if you know what's good for you, stay outa Ma's!" He winked.

Spur tucked on his hat and stepped into the blinding sunlight. According to the telegram he'd received three days ago, Oreville had been a sleepy little town after the gold fury had passed. But in the last three weeks the post office had been robbed twice, both times on the night before the mail was to go out with the stage. Two men had also been killed.

The local mine owner—one Cleve Magnus—had

lost thousands of dollars when the silver ingots he'd been sending to New York had been stolen. The wealthy man had hired four guards to protect the post office. It hadn't been broken into but last week the stagecoach carrying the mail—and Magnus' silver—had been attacked, the driver and gunmen killed, and every last piece of mail stolen. The strongbox was also taken.

The passengers—two women—had been spared. Seems the thieves couldn't bring themselves to shoot them. They're still in town at the Eastern Heights Hotel, which is why Spur had hired a room there.

That was all he'd learned from his boss back in Washington. No possible suspects, nothing else. The Secret Service had a new job for Spur McCoy: find the men responsible for the murders and the thefts and haul them in.

He had little to go on. No one who had seen the men's faces had lived. From what General Halleck had written there were two men doing the robberies.

A young man strolled down the street. "Excuse me!" Spur yelled.

"Huh?" The boy stared at him, glassy-eyed, his nose red with burst capillaries.

"Where could I find the mayor?"

"Old Kincaid?" The youth snorted and threw his hat onto the ground. "Ma's place? Naw. Eatin'? Naw. Screwing a horse? Naw." He scratched his wild-haired hair. "Drinkin'? Naw. Skinny dippin'? Naw. Screwin' a—"

"Do you know where he is?"

The drunken boy shrugged and reeled on

unsteady feet. "You could try his shack. It's right there." He pointed.

McCoy smiled. "That's the livery stable."

"Huh?" The kid moved his gaze from his shoulder, along his arm and out from his fingertip. "Oh yeah. Um, hell! Where'd he put it?" He turned to Spur, curling his upper lip. "Why the hell'd you ask me all these questions?"

"Never mind. I'll find it."

"Then I think I'll take a nap." The young man crumpled onto the street onto a pile of horse droppings and snoozed.

Spur shook his head, asked a well dressed man, and quickly found Mayor Kincaid's home.

He knocked at the handsome two-storey house. No answer. Another knock finally brought a vision to the door—a young woman swathed with peach silk.

"Yes?" she said, primping her hair. "Sorry, I just took off my bonnet. I feel naked."

"Looks fine to me." He smiled at her expression. "I mean, I'm inquiring after Mayor Kincaid, Miss—"

"I'm Kelly Kincaid, the mayor's daughter. *Miss* Kincaid. My father's out somewhere, think he rode to Mr. Magnus' mine about something or t'other." The blonde woman broke into a smile. "My, you must be new in town."

He grinned at the beautiful young woman. "That's a fact. How'd you know?"

Kelly curled a lock of blonde hair around her little finger. "I'd remember you." She giggled and lowered her eyes, but not to Spur's feet.

He could feel her staring at him down there.

Three seconds of that made his pants uncomfortably tight. "Ah, well, Miss Kincaid—"

"Kelly." She looked up into his eyes. "Call me Kelly. Heck, call me anything you want!"

She was so delicious, so willing, but she was the mayor's daughter. "Uh, right, Kelly." Spur stepped back from the threshold. "Know when he'll be back?"

"Not for hours. It's a long ride out to the mine." Kelly moved toward him. "I'm all alone here in this big, old house, lonely and needing male company." She narrowed her shoulders and licked her lips.

Spur's throat tightened. "I guess I'll try again later."

Kelly pouted. "You're not going to leave me, are you? You just got here!"

"I really should be going."

She sighed. "Alright. Who should I say called for the mayor?"

"McCoy. Spur McCoy."

"Spur? What an unusual first name!" Kelly laughed and grabbed his hand. "Won't you come in for a cup of tea? It's the least I can do for you—and I do mean the least."

The contact of her skin on his was so erotic. Spur felt his control slipping. "Ah—ah—"

The determined young woman pulled him into the house and slammed the door behind him.

"Come on, Spur!" Kelly said.

"Come on, ah, what?" He removed his hat—a bit too late for being in the presence of a lady. A *lady*?

She rolled her blue eyes. "You know perfectly well what I'm talking about. I don't think we should waste any more time. Do you?"

"Time? Waste?" His crotch was unbearably tight.

"Yes!" Her eyes were alive. Kelly released his hand and stood in front of him, panting, her breasts rising and falling, straining against the thin material of her silken dress. "I've never beheld a man who did this to me, who could make me feel this way."

"Well, ah, Kelly, ah—"

"Can't you see I'm on fire?" she asked him, and tilted back her head.

He could see it alright. And he liked what he saw. The uninhibited young woman had set a blaze in his body as well. Spur took a stumbling step toward the woman, right there in the parlor.

The door banged open. "Kelly! Did that—oh, hello!"

Spur recovered his balance before he fell onto his face. Flushed, he turned and took in the short, dusty man who stood in the doorway. "Hello yourself," he said in slightly husky voice. "Mayor Kincaid?"

"Yep."

"Spur McCoy."

They shook hands. Spur fanned his face with his Stetson. "You order all this hot weather just for me?"

Kincaid laughed jovially and kissed a suddenly poised Kelly's cheek. "Nope. Heck, McCoy, we're having a cool wave. Normally, it'd be 112 by now." He hung his hat and coat on a rack beside the door. "I was just going out to the mine—Magnus' silver mine—when old Isabella threw a shoe. Had to come right back. Course, there wasn't much I could tell him anyway." Kincaid planted his hands on his hips. "I see you met my daughter."

Kelly beamed. "I was just going to make tea. Would you like a cup, dear father?"

Kincaid rubbed his sweaty face. "Might as well. I have some business to discuss with McCoy here."

"Fine. I'll be right back!" Kelly winked at Spur from behind her father's back and swirled away.

Kincaid led the Secret Service agent into his office. "Glad to see you made it to my little town in one piece, McCoy."

"No problem."

"Ain't it a regular Eden around here? An oasis?"

Spur grinned and lowered his voice. "It's a blooming garden."

Kincaid laughed out loud.

"Had any more robberies lately, Mayor Kincaid? Silver robberies? My information's three days old."

"Nope." The man lit a cheroot and puffed. "But the post office is too well guarded now, and the eastern stage isn't due to leave for a week yet. I don't figure anything'll happen until then."

"I suppose Magnus will put guards on the stage from now on. Right?"

"You can bet the farm on that. He's stocking the coach with gunmen. Cleve is determined not to lose another shipment of his silver."

"Where's he sending it?"

"A big bank back East. He doesn't trust our puny local bank. Sure, he keeps a small account. But the rest of it he ships out as soon as he can."

Spur nodded. Justin Kincaid seemed a reasonable, intelligent man, McCoy thought, as he watched him puff away. He liked him. In one sense he was glad the mayor had walked in when he did. If he'd arrived back home a few minutes later he would have found McCoy and his daughter in a comprising situation, and position.

"You talked with the two female witnesses yet?"

Spur shook his head. "I only just got into town and wanted to see you first."

Kincaid nodded. "You know there's no law around here. The last sheriff quit a year ago when the biggest gold mine petered out and we haven't elected another one. No interest. And, until a few weeks ago, no real reason. Things were quiet here. Then this started happening." The mayor chewed on the end of the cheroot. "I don't understand it."

"Neither do I. But I'll find the men responsible. Trust me, Kincaid."

"I do. Your boss said you're the best."

Spur grunted.

Justin hesitated and set his smoke in an ashtray. "Did my daughter—well, did Kelly—"

The young woman burst into the room. "Tea, anyone?" she asked, bearing two cups.

Spur smiled as he burned his hands on the cup. Justin Kincaid shrugged at him.

"I'll be in the kitchen if you need me," Kelly said, waltzing out.

"She's quite a woman, that daughter of yours," Spur said.

The mayor spit out his tea.

Five minutes later, Spur walked with Kincaid to the front door.

"Sure hope you can clean up this little problem of ours," Justin said, removing his coat and hat from the rack. "Cleve Magnus is ready to shoot me if he doesn't stop losing his silver, and he's not a violent man." Kincaid opened the front door.

"Mayor! Mayor Kincaid!"

It was the drunken youth Spur had met in the street. Suddenly, he'd had no problem finding Kincaid's home. He reeked of alcohol and pulsed with excitement.

"What is it, Ephraim?"

"Ole Jake Connelly's holed up in a room at Ma's with two girls." The boy gasped. "Says he won't let 'em out until you get over there and forgive him for his carnal sins!"

"What?" Kincaid guffawed.

"It's true! Ma's hunkering around mad as a wet hen. She sent me out here herself." Gasp. Breathe. "You gotta get over there. The guy's gotta knife!"

"The damn fool!" Justin Kincaid turned to Spur. "He thinks I'm a damned priest!"

"Drunker than a skunk he is," said the inebriated youth. "Hurry up! Wait any more and those two girls—Kitty and Felicia—won't be giving you or me any more discounts, mayor!"

Kincaid gave him a stern look and shrugged on his coat. "Okay. Okay! Sorry, McCoy. Duty calls. I'll be back as soon as I can untangle things."

He ran out the door ahead of the sweating youth.

Kelly walked up beside Spur. "What was all that about?" she asked, peering through the doorframe.

He smiled. "Your father's, ah, needed elsewhere."

"Good. Because I need you here." Kelly Kincaid slid her hand between his legs.

CHAPTER THREE

"Look, young lady. You are the mayor's daughter." Spur McCoy flushed as he gently peeled Kelly Kincaid's fingers from his crotch.

"Uh-huh." She wrestled from his grip and zeroed in on her target once again.

Spur flinched at the erotic contact. "He could come back here any time."

"Yes."

He backed away from her, inadvertently closing the door. "He'd be mad as heck if he saw what you're doing right—uh, oh—now."

"Positively livid." The blonde-haired woman fingered him below his brass belt buckle.

He caught her gaze, smiled, and let her work him over. "We really shouldn't be doing this. You're so young."

"Eighteen," Kelly said, furiously stroking the growing bulge between his legs.

"Really?" He groaned.

"Yes."

"Well then—" Spur shook his head. "Kelly, stop that!"

She used both hands, sliding them up and down his thighs and gripping the most sensitive part of his body. She was at him like a Pagan at an idol.

"You hear me, girl? You better stop that or I'll let you have it!"

Kelly squeezed him so hard that Spur's body convulsed. His head smacked into the kerosene lamp that hung adjacent to the front door.

"That does it. Come with me, young lady!" McCoy grabbed her hand, but she laughed, twisted away from him and ran up the stairs.

Spur followed her flying skirt and petticoats, taking two steps at a time, but she was fast. He didn't catch up with her until the girl had cleared a hallway and had disappeared inside a room.

"Kelly?" he said as he walked in.

Mayor Kincaid's daughter pounced on him from behind the door. The delicious attack threw him off balance. McCoy crashed onto the canopied feather bed as the girl giggled and laughed and rolled over his body.

Spur relaxed and gasped. Kelly was all over him, kissing, groping. She lay fully on top of him and rubbed her groin against him. The pressure at his crotch increased tenfold. Spur grabbed her head and pulled it closer.

He forced his tongue between her lips and sank it into the young woman's mouth. She ground her breasts against his chest and moaned as she took McCoy's thrusts, stabbing her own tongue between her parted teeth.

Kelly threw back her head and gasped.

"Let me guess. I'm your first man," Spur said, fumbling with the tiny white buttons that extended down the back of her silk dress.

"No time for small talk, Spur!" Kelly slid off him, bent and ripped open his belt.

He was halfway down her back when the mayor's daughter succeeded in hauling his pants and under-drawers down to his thighs. Kelly went crazy at the sight of his genitals, peppering them with kisses, licking and tasting everything in sight until Spur had to pull her mouth from him.

"Hold on, girl!" he said as the impending explosion subsided within him. "Jeez! You're worse than a—a—than anything I've ever seen!"

She looked up at him with glassy eyes. Locks of blonde hair veiled her face. "Spur, I've never wanted a man as much as I want you!"

He opened the last button. They looked at each other for a second and clambered off the bed.

Spur pulled off his boots, pants and under-drawers as Kelly removed her dress. Seconds later they were stark naked, rolling over and over on the carpeted floor, locked in a wet, plunging kiss.

He pumped his hips against her mound. Their bodies nudged the dresser so they reversed direc-tion. Spur held her to the carpet and took her aroused nipples in his mouth, one at a time, left then right, slurping the succulent morsels with just enough of a bite to drive the woman wild.

The heat slickened their bodies. Kelly pushed him away and slammed him onto his back. She took him in her hand. Spur closed his eyes as the incredible sensation washed over him.

"You're good," he said as her blonde mane bobbed between his legs. "Oh, god—make that *real* good!"

The tight, wet, constricting feeling energized him. Oblivious to the intense heat, the open bedroom door and the dangerous situation he was in, Spur surrendered to the woman with the magic throat.

Up she went. All the way down. Again and again. He groaned and bucked his hips up to meet her liquid lips. Kelly pulled at his scrotum and sucked him with obvious relish for two minutes, slowing when he was on the verge, speeding when he'd regained control, repeating the cycle until he was out of his mind.

Spur helplessly groaned.

Kelly pulled off him with a loud pop and looked into his eyes. "Had enough, big boy? And I do mean big!"

Spur took her head in his hands. "I don't care if you are Mayor Kincaid's daughter," he said, his voice husky. "I'm gonna ram you, but good!"

She stretched out on her back, spread her legs and lifted her hips. "I don't care if I'm Mayor Kincaid's daughter either. Just do it. Do it to me!"

Their bodies fit together. Spur thrust into her, gently at first, then harder. Staring into her eyes, holding onto her hips, he pushed himself full-length into her.

Kelly's mouth hung open in the erotic expression of a woman who hasn't been with a man for awhile. She clutched his back and moaned, shivering, rubbing her hardened nipples across his hairy chest.

"I'm glad I didn't save myself for marriage."

He pulled out and slammed back into Kelly.

She winced. "Or become a nun."

Another pump.

The woman blinked. Her face flushed. "Or—or—ah hell, Spur! That's so good!"

He grinned at her. Their hip bones crashed together. The oak bed creaked. Spur pounded into the young woman whose astonished stares were periodically broken by moans. They sank deeper into the thick feather mattress.

Kelly held onto his hairy thighs, writhing and twisting, meeting his stroking hips. She squeezed around him to increase their mutual pleasure, breathing faster and faster.

She was so beautiful, so willing, that Spur felt himself losing control. He slowed down.

"Damnit, McCoy!" Kelly said. "I was almost there!" She dug her fingernails into his ass. "Do it as hard as you can! Jesus, let me have it all the way!"

He did, driving into her with quick, deep thrusts. Kelly wailed and urged him on with her hands. Spur mindlessly plowed between her legs, lost in an erotic world of warm, sweet flesh.

The mattress exploded. White feathers squirted out around them on both sides. Spur got onto his hands and toes and continued to plunge into her. The increased stimulation freed Kelly from that trembling moment of hesitation. She screamed and thrashed beneath him.

That did it. Spur had no choice. The room went blank. He exploded, spastically jabbing into her, grunting, kissing her forehead, revelling in the primal male feeling of seed spurting from his body.

His tight-muscled form vibrated and shook. Kelly moaned as he pumped into her again and again, stroking his back, clamping her legs around him, catching her breath in her throat. Spur finally sank onto her, spent, useless. They kissed as feathers floated down onto them from the air.

He snoozed for a minute or two, only to wake up to Kelly's laughter.

Spur opened his eyes and kissed her. "What— what's so funny?"

"You. You look like a chicken!" Kelly convulsed with giggles.

"Huh?" He twisted around and saw the feathers that had adhered to his sweaty back. Spur smiled back at her. "I'm the rooster. You're the chicken."

"Right. I never can remember which is which."

"Sure, Kelly. Sure."

She wiped off the feathers as he dressed. After their moment together, once his mind had cleared, Spur was anxious to get on with his mission. As much as he'd enjoyed it, he had work to do. He put on his professional attitude.

"Here!" Kelly said. "Don't forget your hat!"

McCoy took it from her with a kiss. "Ah, sorry about the room," he said, gesturing to the ruined mattress and the thousands of white clumps covering the floor.

"Not to worry," Kelly said. "It was worth it. You'll be back to see me before you leave town, right?"

"Right. I promise."

One last kiss and Spur was out the bedroom door. Fortunately, he didn't meet Justin Kincaid on his exit from the man's house. Spur smiled. Nothing like a midday romp in the hay to get him eager for work. Or, more correctly, a romp in the feathers.

He went to the Eastern Heights Hotel. The two women passengers who'd witnessed the stagecoach robbery were registered in room 23. They hadn't been cooperative with the Mayor's investigation but Spur knew they had something that would help.

Finding the room, he knocked.

"Go away!"

The female's voice didn't sound friendly. Undaunted, he banged again. "I'm here to help you!" McCoy said, trying to remember the women's names.

"Here to kill us, more likely!"

"No!"

Silence.

"Come on, ma'am! Just want to talk with you. Mayor Kincaid sent me here." He tried the knob. Locked.

"Well . . . ."

He heard feet shuffling in the room, the sound of women's boots against bare wood.

"How do I know you're not one of them men who attacked the stagecoach?"

"Ma'am, Mrs. Grieve, just open the door."

A key turned. The knob twisted. An elderly woman peered at him, her face pinched beneath the lace bonnet, eyes steely and active.

"Well?" she asked.

He removed his hat. "I'm Spur McCoy. Mayor Kincaid called me into town to investigate these robberies, including the one you were unfortunately involved with. May I come in?"

Emma Grieve shook her head. "Not yet. What do you want to know?"

"Everything, Mrs. Grieve, it would be so much easier for all of us if you'd just let me—" '

"Okay. Alright!"

Spur walked in as she stepped aside. The hotel room was identical to his own, save for the laces and petticoats strewn over every piece of furniture. A young girl with sad eyes huddled in a chair, meticulously working on a piece of embroidery. The girl was pretty, with a pert nose, huge blue eyes and ringlets of brown hair. Her face showed the last traces of the sunburn that she'd obviously received during her recent ordeal.

The old woman slammed the door behind him and locked it. "Hurry up. We don't got all day, mister!"

He turned to her—the girl's grandmother, if he remembered correctly. "Fine. Did you—"

"Save your breath, mister." Emma Grieve shook her head. "Can't remember a thing except that one man screaming at us the whole time, telling us he was going to kill us and leave us there for the blizzards to eat us up."

"Buzzards?" Spur guessed.

She frowned. "Blizzards, buzzards. See, I told you I can't remember!" The old woman walked to the girl. "Melissa here hasn't been the same since that day." Her face softened. "Neither have I for that matter. Had to walk five miles back to this hell-hole of a town after those animals left us alone in the desert. My arthritis flared up something fierce. Sorry, mister, we can't help you. Go away and leave us alone!"

"Were the men wearing kerchiefs over their faces?"

"I don't know. Yes, I guess so." Emma Grieve put a hand on Melissa's shoulder.

"And there were two of them?"

She nodded. Mrs. Grieve smiled tightly. "Now I'll have to ask you to leave again. And don't come back!"

"Thanks for your time, ladies." Spur sighed as Emma Grieve unlocked and opened the door.

"Find them."

The small, high voice behind him made McCoy turn back just as he stepped from the room. Melissa Grieve didn't look up at him.

"Now you shush, Melissa. Time to put some more cream onto those burns." Emma pointed into the hall. "Good day, mister!"

A rifle exploded in the hall, sending a messenger of death flying into the women's room.

CHAPTER FOUR

Spur McCoy ducked as hot lead slammed into the hotel room's wall.

"Lock the door and stay there!" he yelled to Emma and Melissa. As he dashed out of the room, drawing his revolver, Spur caught a glimpse of two men flying down the stairs.

His boots pounded the floorboards. McCoy powered along the hall. He skidded, grabbed the railing on each side and half-ran, half-slid down the stairway. The gunmen disappeared outside, leaving the hotel's front door wide open.

Pumping his arms, he sped across the deserted lobby and rushed onto the porch, ready to fire, searching for a target.

The street was empty of people. A few horses drank at the trough in front of the Eastern Heights Hotel. A man wearing a minister's collar wiped sweat from his forehead as he trudged along with an armful of bibles. No one else was in sight. No sign of the two gunmen.

"Reverend!" Spur said, dashing up to the man of the cloth. "Two gunmen just ran out of the hotel. Must have gone right past you. Did you see them?"

The bespectacled man stared up at him above his unwieldly cargo. "No, my son. Nothing but the glory of this day that the Lord has made."

Spur was running before the man finished his sentence. He checked the wide alleys between the stores. He rushed straight through the livery stable. He searched through the piles of costly, imported timber stacked behind the "Fine Construction Supplies" building.

Nothing!

Spur stopped in the middle of the street, panting, his shirt soaked to the skin, fidgeting with his weapon. Where the hell had the men gone?

The barber who'd chopped off his hair earlier that day called to him from his shop.

"Who's dead?" Blair asked, hesitantly venturing from his place of business. "Or, who needs a bullet dug out?"

"No one. Damn! Two men just took a potshot at me and two ladies in the Eastern Heights Hotel! Seen them?"

The barber rubbed his face and sighed. "Nope. You and two ladies?" Blair chuckled. "At least you're staying away from Ma's place."

"Where the hell is everyone?" Spur asked, waving at the deserted street.

"Aint' much gunfighting in Oreville no more," the barber said, wiping his hands on his blue pants. "When a man decides to start shooting, citizens make themselves scarce."

"Great. So no one saw them." He dug his toe into the inch-thick dust that covered Main Street.

Blair shrugged. "If I'm not needed, guess I'll feed the dog." He walked back into his shop.

The two men who'd fired into Emma and Melissa's room had to be the same pair who'd robbed the eastbound stagecoach. They hadn't been after him. They'd been trying to silence them, Spur figured. He holstered his revolver.

But why do it in the middle of the day? It didn't make any sense. Unless—unless they weren't professionals. Unless they were experimenting around.

Or unless they weren't too smart.

As he stood there, thinking it through, Oreville returned to as much life as it could muster. Men appeared from the saloons, mounted up and rode off. Women walked with pails to the nearby river for water. Two boys in clean short pants—city clothes—threw rocks at each other.

Spur asked every passerby if they'd seen the gunmen, but no one had. They didn't seem to be lying, he decided. They simply hadn't.

He walked back to the hotel. The lobby was still empty, the manager nowhere in sight. On the second floor he knocked on room 23.

"It's me, Mrs. Grieve. Spur McCoy!"

"You git your butt outta here!" the elderly woman shrieked. "You sent those men to kill us!"

"No, I didn't!" Spur yelled back. "Use some sense, Mrs. Grieve."

"Sense? I'f I'd used sense I wouldn't have a hole in my wall and a shaking granddaughter! Now git before I blow you to hell with this rifle of mine!"

Spur started to knock again but heard the unmistakable sound of a rifle being loaded.

"Okay. But I'll be back."

He turned and walked to his room. Spur needed to sit down and do some thinking.

"You idiots!" Julie Golden said. She planted her hands on her hips. "How could you be so stupid? How? Answer me!"

Carl Mond and Jedidiah Steele stood with their hats in their hands and stared at the woman's kitchen floor.

"I told you to shoot them at two!" she continued, grilling them with her green-tinted gaze.

"But it was two, ma'am," Carl said in a low voice.

Julie slapped her bosom. "Two in the morning, not two in the afternoon!" She circled them. "What were you thinking, going into that hotel with your guns drawn, ready to do your dirty work while the sun's still up, in front of the whole wide world?"

"Well, I, uh—" Carl looked at Jed, who shook his head.

She sighed. "Did anyone see you running back here? I don't want to be connected with this."

"Certainly not, Miss Golden!" Mond pulled in his chin. "We're smart enough not to do that."

"I see. You just can't tell time." Julie shook her head. "Never mind. I'll take care of it my way." Julie had done her best to sound as fierce and angry as she should have felt. Inside, though, she could barely hide her relief that the man hadn't carried out the orders she'd passed onto them from Lionel Kemp.

"Okay. Stop standing there like a coupla boys who've messed your pants! You better lie low for a while. Stay here. Keep the doors and windows locked. Don't show yourselves in town, you hear? Heavens, you didn't even cover your faces!"

Carl burped.

Julie Golden tied the bonnet onto her head and adjusted it by feel. "It might be better this way," she said.

The two men glanced up at her.

"What—what you got in mind, Miss Golden?" Carl asked.

"Yeah, what?"

Julie reached for the kitchen door. "You'll find out soon enough. Just don't leave until I get back. Those girls will drop out of sight."

She strode down Camp Street, her boots kicking up the dirt that she hated so much. But Julie smiled as she walked to the Eastern Heights Hotel.

She'd figured Carl and Jed would be too dumb to do the right thing. She'd given them a stunning performance, telling them that the two women had told Mayor Kincaid that they'd identify the men tomorrow morning who'd robbed the stagecoach. Then Julie had told them that Emma and Melissa Grieve had to die as soon as possible. "At two," she'd told them. "And make sure you're not seen!"

Just as she'd planned, they'd gone ahead and hustled out to the women's room an hour later.

Lionel Kemp might have her livelihood wrapped around his finger but she wasn't his slave. There were things she could do, things he'd never dream of.

She hoped everything would go smoothly.

Julie Golden stopped in front of the hotel, stamped the dust from her black boots, smoothed her skirt and walked inside. It was just about summer time, after all, and she couldn't bear the thought of cooking.

A strange sight greeted her in the hotel's dining room. Five men stood with revolvers and rifles across their chests, backs to the wall, guarding the diners. They stared at Julie as she walked in.

The long table was empty save for an elderly woman and her young charge. She'd spot them anywhere, though she'd never seen them. Those had to be the two.

Julie seated herself across from the women.

"Good afternoon," she said, smiling.

The girl's hand shook as she lifted a fork to her mouth. The elderly woman nodded to her.

"Guess I'm not late for supper," Julie said, staring at the huge bowls of vegetables and the platter of still-steaming roast beef.

Once again the two women didn't speak.

They must have had a real fright, Julie thought, and she didn't blame them for acting like they were.

She leaned across the table. "Listen, ladies, I know all about your situation, and I think I can help."

Emma shook her head and murmured something into her glass of red wine.

"I know you can't leave Oreville until you can make up the money that was stolen from you on the stagecoach last week."

Melissa dropped her fork.

"Miss," Emma Grieve said, finally looking up at Julie. "You're upsetting the child."

"I'm sorry, but I heard about what happened, and I've figured out a way for you to get out of here as soon as possible. Interested?"

Emma nodded.

"I know it costs a small fortune to take the stage. Then you have to buy a ticket for the railroad. But I can get you the money. You can be back home in a week. Two weeks at most!"

Melissa picked up her fork and glanced hopefully at her grandmother. Mrs. Grieve set her glass on the table and studied the woman who was beaming at them.

She almost spoke, parted her lips and turned toward the guards behind her. "Okay, men. Thanks for protecting us. Those three killers won't be back. But stay outside the door just in case, will you?"

"Of course, Mrs. Grieve!" a burly man said.

The five shuffled out and closed the dining room door.

"I don't know why, you should care about us," Emma said. "We're strangers to you."

Julie smiled. "Why shouldn't I care? I'm a woman just like you. I was in a bad situation a few months back and someone helped me. It's simple."

Emma Grieve's lower lip trembled. "No one can help us. We're all alone. No relations, no friends. No one. All we have is each other."

Julie reached across the roast beef and clasped the woman's wrinkled hand. "You've got me! And I can get you out of Oreville. Guaranteed!"

She brightened but bit her unpainted lower lip. "Our kind don't cotton to charity," Emma slowly said.

Julie had caught the glimmer. The light of hope

in her eyes. "Who said anything about charity? I'm talking about work. You'll earn the money fair and square."

"I've done washing and scrubbing," Melissa said, turning her reddened face toward Julie.

"Well, it'll be something like that. Then it's settled. You two done with your dinner?"

Emma pushed away her place and wiped her lips. "Yes, we are. When can we get started?"

"Right now. Shall we go?"

Julie led them from the room, past the guards and out of the hotel. Dusk settled in on the town as they walked two blocks south on Main and turned down Fletcher.

"This street was named after the man who first discovered gold in the hills. Did you know that?" Julie asked conversationally.

"No. Come on, Melissa! Don't hang back! We've got work to do!"

"Don't worry about those men who were after you. I heard they rode out of town."

"That's a load off my chest, pardon the expression," Emma said.

Julie laughed. She turned left past the livery stable and led Emma and Melissa along the tree-choked waterfront, passing the rear of the largest buildings in town.

"Where are you taking us?" Emma asked as her boots sunk into the soft earth.

"My place. Or, one of them at least. You'll see soon enough."

"Oh my god!"

"What is it, Mrs. Grieve?" Julie was suddenly very wary.

"Land sakes, my dear! You're being so kind to us and I don't even know your name!"

She relaxed. "It's Julie. Julie Golden." They halted at the foot of a long, rickety flight of stairs that cut across the back wall of a two storey building. "And here we are. Up you go!" she said gently.

Emma shook her head in the fading light. "My arthritis might argue with you." She clutched the railing.

"Don't worry, Mrs. Grieve. You won't have to use these stairs very often. I just figured it'd be better to bring you in this way. The inside ones are much easier to manage."

They climbed. Melissa patiently followed her slow grandmother. As they rose from the ground, the elderly woman quickened her pace. The sun set below the horizon. An evening breeze ruffled the three women's skirts.

On the landing, Julie produced a key from her sleeve and unlocked the door. She ushered the women inside.

The smell of tobacco smoke, whiskey and cheap perfume hung in the air. The corridor was dark, lit by two lonely kerosene lamps. Fourteen doors led from the hall.

Melissa stared at her grandmother. "What—what kind of place is this?"

Emma turned to Julie as the woman locked the door behind them. "Why, child, this is the kind of place I used to work in. Remember? I told you all about it?" Mrs. Grieve heartily laughed and smiled at Julie. "Of course, that was a long time ago. Years and years back. Mrs. Golden, you are a sly one, you is."

"But I didn't lie to you. After all, where else can a woman make good money? Especially in a town like this?"

Melissa watched with wide eyes as a man walked past them, turned to stare at her and disappeared into room 12.

"Come on you two," Julie said. "Let's go to my office. We have some business to deal with."

"You don't expect me to—" Melissa tugged on her grandmother's sleeve. "Be one of *those* women?"

"Hush, child!" Emma Grieve said as they walked down the hall.

Most of the rooms weren't quiet. Erotic grunts and the sound of flesh slapping together emanated from them. Melissa tightened her grip on the elderly woman's sleeve.

"After all, Melissa. It's nothing you haven't done before. I mean, you're no virgin."

"Grandmother! How could you say that?"

"Because it's true. Stop acting like a little girl. You're all grown up. Act like it. Really, Miss Golden's doing us a favor."

Melissa squeakily cried.

Julie smiled as she unlocked her office. Everything was working out perfectly.

CHAPTER FIVE

"Isn's that him?" Jed Steele asked as he peered out the window at Julie Golden's house.

Carl pushed him away and stared out the slit between the curtains. "Sure as shit is. That's the bugger that was there at the women's hotel room!"

Jed swallowed hard. "Think he saw our faces?"

"I don't know."

"Neither do I."

They watched him wander down the road.

"Maybe we shouldn't take no chances," Carl coughed. "Maybe we should—"

"I don't know. Miss Golden told us to stay put. I don't like the way she looks at us when we mess up. She's liable to shoot us with that derringer of hers!"

"Hell, boy," Mond said, snorting. "You afraid of her?"

"No." His voice was unconvincing.

"Right. C'mon. Use your pea-sized brain! She'd want us to plug that bastard! He's what got us in trouble in the first place! If we take him out she won't be near as sore at us like she just was."

"I guess."

The two men buckled on their gunbelts.

"Your piece fully loaded?" Jed asked.

"Yeah, yeah. Let's get him!"

They walked onto the front porch as dusk spread gloom over Oreville.

The chill in the air refreshed Spur. Even though it had been hours ago he was still searching for the two men who'd come after the female witnesses to the coach robbery. He'd been through most of the town, knocking on doors, talking to every business owner and clerk he could find. Absolutely no one had been able to help him.

This three-block square area of decaying yet opulent houses, obviously built during the gold rush days, was the only section of Oreville he hadn't been through. Spur sighed, walked up to a squat house and knocked on the door.

The door fell inside with an echoing crash, rusted off its hinges. Spur stopped and looked around. How many of these houses were occupied?

Kerosene light glowed in the windows of the house next to it, and in the one down the street. He moved to the monstrous, three story structure.

An explosion rocketed through the night.

Spur slammed face-first to the ground. Hot lead dug into the dust a foot from his head.

Shit!

He slithered over to the nearest cover—an

overturned, weather-worn buggy that had long since outlived its usefulness. The gunman fired two more rounds as McCoy drew.

Make that gun*men*, Spur thought wryly, as the sounds of the new shots were obviously made by a different weapon.

He peered through a hole in the floor of the old buggy. Dusk was melting into night. The shots seemed to have come from directly across the street.

Where was his target?

Another round splintered one of the buggy's axles. Spur clearly saw the flash of gunpowder and pounded two bullets into the area.

No response. He fired a third time, aiming slightly farther to the right.

A volley of ammunition pounded into the buggy. Spur cursed as the top half split off and crashed onto him. His cover was rapidly disappearing.

He threw the wood behind him and peered through a new hole. Still unable to see anything across the street, and knowing that no man could hope for accurate aim at that distance, Spur chanced it. He hunkered down and sped from the buggy to a woodpile beside the three story house.

More shots, more misses.

The woodstack was thick, well packed and perfect for use. With fast, practiced hands, Spur flipped open his revolver's chamber and reloaded with the spares he always kept in his coat pocket. He blasted another round into the area.

It was fully dark. The explosive flashes of the men's return fire showed that they had moved twenty or so feet. The sounds of their weapons richocheted around the abandoned homes.

This wasn't getting either of them anywhere. Who'd be crazy enough to shoot from so far away?

The men who'd messed up at the hotel? Definitely!

Three more rounds dislodged the top few logs from the wood pile, scattering them around him. Spur got a fresh bullet, laid it on top of the pile, set a log just behind it and reloaded.

He slipped back of the house, circled around it, ran up to the front and sped across the inky street, making as little sound as possible.

The unseen gunmen blasted the barely discernible stack of wood. One of their rounds hit the live bullet he'd placed on the stack. The resulting explosion gave the illusion that Spur hadn't moved. He smiled and moved cautiously behind the house where the men had taken up position.

It was a massive thing. Spur took slow, careful steps, careful not to betray his approach. The men stopped firing. He reached the far wall and started toward them.

McCoy flattened himself against the wall and listened. No sound issued from the front of the house. Breathing deeply, his revolver drawn and ready to fire, Spur McCoy lunged out of safety and riddled the area with lead.

He discharged all six rounds and slipped back around the corner, quickly filling the heated chambers with fresh ammunition.

No response.

A sinking feeling rumbled around in his gut. Spur boldly walked into the area.

The men had gone.

He twisted his head in both directions. The darkened street didn't reveal their location.

He'd lost them.

Julie Golden grinned as she unlocked the door to her house, sniffing the odor of gunpowder in the air. Must have been some shooting around here, she thought.

Everything had gone well with Melissa and Emma. She'd assigned them rooms right next to each other. Emma would just stay in her room and Melissa would work.

Of course, she hadn't told them that her guards had been instructed not to let the women leave the saloon. They were trapped and didn't even know it. Not only did she have a new girl but she'd also successfully gotten the women out of the way, for the moment at least.

Lionel Kemp would think they were dead. If necessary, she'd tell him she'd killed the women herself. Her place was off-limits to him anyway; the man would never know.

She'd decide what to do with them later. Now she had Carl and Jed to deal with.

They weren't in the kitchen. "Carl?" she yelled as she closed and locked the door.

Julie's face flushed. If they hadn't stayed there in the house she'd—she'd—

"Up here, ma'am!" a weak voice called from the second floor.

Curious, Julie raced up the curving staircase.

Carl and Jed were sitting back to back, bound together with rope. They turned expressionless faces to her.

"What on earth happened here?" she demanded.

" 'Bout time you got back!"

Lionel Kemp rose from the chair behind the door.

Julie gasped, unable to mask her surprise at seeing the man she hated so much.

Kemp spat. "I never should have trusted a woman to do this job."

"Why not? I haven't done anything wrong!" Julie unbuttoned her ankle length coat. "I've handed over every piece of silver. Every last bit!"

He stared at her with pointy, intense eyes. "That's not what I'm talking about."

"I see. Ah, why'd you tie them up?"

"They're no good, Julie. Just like I warned you. They're piss-poor excuses for men."

She shrugged off her coat and untied her bonnet. "What makes you say that?"

Kemp rolled up his sleeves. "Don't try to outsmart me, woman! You don't have the brains to do it. They tried to kill the women in broad daylight. They just got done shooting up the whole area trying to plug the man who stopped them at the hotel." Lionel spat on the floor. "They're worthless, Julie. Besides. We don't need them anymore."

"We don't?" she asked, glancing at the two men. She didn't like the tone of his voice.

"No." Lionel Kemp stood three feet from her. "I've got new plans."

"Oh." She forced a smile. "So, so pay them off and send them out of town."

"I'll pay them off alright. In the meantime, come on, Julie. Take 'em off. Strip!"

Julie paled. "Now? In front of the men?"

"Come on. Bashful or something all of a sudden?"
He leered at her. "Hell; more men have seen you
naked than have ever seen you wearing a dress! You
were a whore for fifteen years, bitch! Now do it!"

She hesitated.

"Remember, I own you. Lock, stock and barrel."
Lionel stomped to her and held his face an inch
from hers. "Get naked. Now!" he thundered.

Julie shivered as she undressed. Carl and Jed
didn't glance at her, not even when she'd completed
the simple action.

"What now, sir?"

"On the bed. Do it!" he said, rubbing his crotch.
Drool dripped from his lower lip.

Shivering in the breeze blowing through the
windows, Julie went to the bed and sat on the edge
of the mattress.

"On yer back!"

"Lionel, I don't really feel like it right now," she
said, stretching out beside the bound men. Carl's
dirty pants scraped against her thigh as she tried
to get comfortable. Impulsively, she spread her legs.

"You still don't unnerstand, do you, girlie?"
Lionel Kemp shook his head. "It doesn't matter
what you want. You'll do as I say or else!"

He loomed over her, staring down with a tense
face.

"Now, Julie, watch. Watch what happens to
people who don't follow orders."

Lionel produced a Bowie knife from his back
pocket. Julie flinched as the gleaming steel blade
flashed through the air.

"You men aren't worth *shit*!" Lionel said.

Carl tensed. "Please!" he said. "Don't!"

"Shut up!" Lionel looked at the woman. "Watch this. Watch this and remember!"

Carl and Jed kicked on the bed, struggling against the rough rope that bound their hands and torsos. Lionel laughed with relish. He pushed off his hat with his left hand and toyed with the knife as the two men thrashed and pleaded for mercy.

"You're enjoying this, Lionel! You're actually enjoying this!"

He ignored the naked woman. "Check out time, boys. This hotel's closed."

Carl Mond jabbed his boot between Lionel's legs. The big man doubled over and howled in agony as pain shot through his testicles. Julie fought the urge to smile.

"Goddamnit!"

He gasped and shook his head, massaging the damaged tissues. Lionel Kemp plunged the knife into Carl's chest.

"Take that!" he said, as steel pierced bone and flesh and vital organs.

Carl screamed.

Julie cried and turned her head.

The mattress bounced violently as Lionel stabbed Carl Mond, sheathing the knife in his body so hard and so many times that it finally slumped lifelessly against the rope.

"Now for you," he said.

More screams. More bounces. Then nothing.

Julie held back the revulsion that rose within her. She breathed through her mouth to avoid the horrid smell of death. Tears squeezed from her eyelids.

Grunting, panting, Lionel grabbed her head with bloody hands.

"Look at me, goddamnit!"

She opened her eyes.

"If you don't want to be next, do exactly what I say. Is that clear, girlie?"

It was.

CHAPTER SIX

Just after the shooting, Spur stood in the light in front of the Motherlode Saloon, shaking his head. He really could use a whiskey, he told himself, even though he wasn't much of a drinker.

McCoy saw a familiar face walking toward him.

"Kincaid!" he yelled. "Mayor Kincaid!"

"And stay out!" a male voice roared from the Motherlode.

"Goddamn shit-faced sumbitch!" an airborne man said as he was pitched from the saloon and plowed into Spur. McCoy slammed his left leg to the ground to support his body. The drunk slid onto the dirt.

"McCoy!" the mayor asked as he stepped over the drunk, "you know anything about all that shooting?"

"Yeah. As it happened, I did some of it."

Justin Kincaid shook his head. "Ever since you

came into town ammunition sales are up by fifty percent. What was it this time?"

The ousted drunk got to his knees, wiped the dirt from his face, groaned and crawled onto the corner of the boardwalk fronting the hotel. He promptly snoozed.

"I was out knocking on doors, searching for someone who'd admit that they'd seen the two men running from the Eastern Heights Hotel after the shooting earlier today. Just after it got dark, two men started firing at me. Never saw them. I returned fire for a while then tried to surprise them. By that time they were gone. Vanished into the darkness."

"I see." Kincaid moved into the light that spilled from the saloon's batwing doors.

"I figure it's the same men I was looking for. They just found me before I found them."

"You mean the ones that almost killed Emma and Melissa Grieve? I heard about it. They must be powerfully bad shots to have missed you. After all, they had the valuable advantage of surprise."

"Distance," Spur said. "Too far for any real accuracy. That's why I couldn't hit either of them, even when I pinpointed their location from the gunpowder flashes."

Kincaid nodded and looked inside the saloon. "You, ah, riding out to Cleve Magnus' mine tomorrow?"

Spur nodded thoughtfully. "Think it's time I paid the man a visit."

"Good. Stop by and see me. I'll give you directions." He glanced inside the building. "Well, I should be going in. Have to see Ma. Strictly business, of course."

Spur laughed and put up his hands. "Of course. You're the mayor, after all."

"Yeah. Right."

A buxom young woman walked from the saloon, holding up the left shoulder of her dress.

"Justin!" she said smiling. "Justin, this big-handed oaf ripped up the new dress I bought this morning! See?" She released the cloth. It dropped away, revealing her bare shoulder and half of her left breast. "All my other dresses are out to be cleaned. Ma's not here so she can't help me. I can't go around like this all night, can I?" She turned to Spur. "Well? What do you think?"

He grinned. "Depends on if you're gonna wear the rest of it or not."

The woman smiled. "Justin, dear heart, is Gertie still at her shop?"

"Ah, I doubt it, Michelle." The mayor fidgeted as the woman grabbed his arm.

She dropped her sweet girl ploy. "Dangit! That seamstress'll charge me double if I call at her house, especially after sundown!"

Two cowboys whistled at the woman as they walked into the saloon. One of them slapped her rump. The whore squealed in delight.

"Look, Michelle, maybe I can help you out. But cover yourself, my dear. Don't want the men of this town thinking you're a loose woman."

"But I am, Justin! You know that better than anyone within a hundred miles." She smirked but pulled up the front of her dress, concealing that portion of her offendingly delicious anatomy.

Spur smiled at the mayor's obvious discomfort.

"Sorry, McCoy. Duty, ah, calls."

"Of course. I could use some sleep. I'll see you in the morning, mayor."

"Sure."

"Oh, honey, your friend ain't comin' in with you?" Gertie asked. "The show starts in just a few minutes."

"Sorry, ma'am. I'll be leaving now."

"Ma'am. Ma'am?" Michelle shook her head. "Such manners! Then come on, Justin. I've got something to show you. Ma just bought me a nice new set of ropes and chaps!"

Spur laughed as the mayor hustled the whore into the saloon. He returned to his hotel for a much-needed dose of sleep.

Julie Golden hadn't been surprised when Lionel had changed his mind about bedding her. Not only had Carl managed to temporarily put *that* out of commission with his boot, but the bed was a mess. She glanced at the two lifeless forms that lay there and at the brick-red stains that covered the quilt her mother had sewn for her in her youth.

Lionel Kemp snorted and swung on a bottle of whiskey. "I'm leaving. Leaving town."

She looked at him in shock. Though he'd stayed in Oreville, Lionel had lain low, rarely moving around when anyone could see him. He'd told everyone he was leaving and no one had suspected. "Where are you going? When? For how long?"

"West, in the morning and I don't know." He spat on the floor.

Julie's mind filled with ideas. If he was gone long enough she could cash in her business, clear out her bank account and be gone before he returned to Oreville. She'd take the next stage coach, east or west, and find her fortune elsewhere. Anywhere but Oreville!

"I see."

Lionel Kemp took another swig. "Things are getting too hot around here for my tastes. Besides, I got some investing to do. All that silver sitting there doing nothing. And don't think about runnin' out on me. If you do I'll track you down and kill you myself!"

Julie stared quietly at him. "I see."

"Cheer up, darling. You know you'll miss me, but I'll be back soon. I hope you can handle things here alone. I'll be sending you telegrams every day, telling you what to do. And you better have carried out my orders when I return. If not—" He nodded toward the dead men.

She hugged herself, suddenly cold.

"Besides, I wouldn't have to actually do anything to you. All I have to do is have lunch with Mayor Kincaid. Or hand Cleve Magnus a rifle and point him in your direction."

"Alright. Alright! Leave town!" she said, exploding. "I'll be a good little girl. Don't you worry about me." Julie hardened her voice. It was easy; she'd had so much practice. "What's next on your Christmas list? Robbing little old ladies? Maybe the fund for the church building?"

He raised his eyebrows. "Interesting. I knew you had potential—even if you are a woman."

"Come on, Lionel! I've done things for you that most men wouldn't do."

He snorted and guffawed.

Her cheeks reddened. "I don't mean—"

"Just keep yer skirts clean, girlie." Lionel planted his hat on his head and walked toward the bedroom door.

"What am I supposed to do with those bodies?" Julie demanded.

"You'll think of something." Lionel kept on walking.

"Okay. Okay! Jesus!" Spur yelled as he stumbled from the bed and answered the insistent knock.

"Open up, McCoy! You awake?"

"I don't know if I'm alive." He barked his shins on the chair. "That you, Kincaid?" He turned the key in the lock and swung open the door.

"Yes!" The mayor was breathing hard.

Spur yawned. "What the hell time is it?"

"After eight, but that's not important." He pushed past Spur. "McCoy, a prospector found two bodies in the desert this morning just after sunrise."

He rubbed his eyes. "Bodies?"

"That's what he says."

"So?"

"Tarnation, man! Wake up! The two men who shot at you last night. Remember them? They might have wound up dead in the desert."

"Could be them, or a couple million others."

Kincaid shook his head. "Nope. The prospector said it looked like they'd been taken there. Stabbed to death but almost no blood on the ground."

"So?" Spur couldn't shake the fuzz from his head.

Mayor Kincaid sighed, grabbed the ewer from the table, poured some water into the basin and motioned to Spur. "Come over here."

"Huh?" McCoy looked at him with one eye.

Kincaid gripped the Secret Service agent's shoulders, bent him at the waist and struck his face into the water. Spur bubbled and gasped but it did the trick. He forced his head from the basin and wiped his face.

"Better now?" Kincaid asked.

"Yeah. Thanks." Spur toweled himself off. "When're we going out to look at these bodies?"

The mayor threw Spur his gunbelt. "Right now."

Spur dressed. The horse that the mayor provided him with was fast, lean and eagerly responded to his commands. On their way out of town they rode down a familiar street.

"That's where I had that run-in last night," Spur said, pointing to the abandoned house. The bullet holes were plainly visible around its front door.

"Not many folks live in this part of town anymore," Kincaid said.

They rode west over harsh, dry land. It was still cool but the sun quickly built in strength. A half-hour later Kincaid slowed his mount.

"Has to be around here somewhere," the mayor said. "Right over there's Mick's claim."

"How about that? Looks suspicious." Spur pointed to a pile of dead bushes.

"Yeah."

They rode the fifteen feet and dismounted. The two dead men lay face up on the ground surrounded by dried sagebrush. Kincaid looked closer and Spur sighed.

"I'll be a sonofabitch!" he said.

"You know them?" Spur asked.

"Sure! Used to come into Ma's all the time. Loved

the women, those boys did. And never wanted me to forgive them for their sins." He grunted. "Haven't seen them around lately. I figured they'd left town."

"I know them too," Spur said. "At least I think I do. I only saw them for a second but I'd swear those are the men from the hotel."

"The ones who were after Emma and Melissa?"

Spur nodded.

Kincaid stood back and crossed his arms. "So they were after the only living witnesses to the stagecoach robbery and now they're dead. Don't make sense."

McCoy scratched his stubbly chin. "Unless they were working for someone else."

Kincaid looked hard at him.

"They robbed the stage. They probably robbed the post office, killed the Chinese man and the young kid who happened along at the wrong times. If they were working for someone else, that man might have decided they'd outlived their usefulness and put them out of business."

"Yeah, I follow you. But why dump them way out here?" Kincaid pushed back his hat and wiped his forehead. "Haven't been dead too long. Must've happened last night or early this morning."

"The killer might have hoped that no one would find them for a while. Might have thought it was wiser not to stir up any more trouble in town."

"After all that shooting last night, I can imagine."

Spur studied the bodies. "Kincaid, who'd have the most to gain from robbing Magnus' silver shipments?"

The mayor laughed. "Every man, woman and

child in town. Times are hard since the mines closed."

"What about the men who work for Cleve Magnus? They must have some loot."

"Sure do. But they live out at the mine. Come into town once or twice a week and spend up a storm. They're what's keeping Oreville alive. He must have fifty men out there." Kincaid paused. "Folks are still packing up and leaving town. More than half the houses are empty. Stores are closing. I've even had to talk the blacksmith into staying so we'll have someone to make tools. Oreville's slowly dying."

"Sorry about that," Spur said. "How far away is this Magnus mine?"

Kincaid pointed to the range of rugged mountains which looked deceptively close. "About an hour's ride due east," he said.

Spur nodded and walked to his horse. "Think I'll head out there." He checked his canteen which the mayor had hung from his borrowed mount's saddle. It was full.

"Good luck, McCoy. I'll get these bodies into town."

"And thanks for the use of the horse." Spur stepped onto the brown mare.

"No problem. Just remember to bring her back in one piece."

Spur laughed and rode off toward the distant mine.

He let the cooperative mount walk the first few miles, but gradually urged her faster and faster over the rock-strewn, cactus-covered ground. The mountains gradually approached him but Spur soon realized that Kincaid had misjudged the amount of time it would take to get there.

The sun was an hour later in the sky by the time he stopped and took a drink. The mare snorted at the smell of water, so Spur poured some of the precious liquid into his hat and let her drink.

Refreshed from the stop, he rode again. A lighter colored area slashing across the shoulder of a huge mountain ahead showed where men had moved rocks and earth, exposing the underyling dirt that hadn't been covered with desert varnish. Must be Cleve Magnus' mine, he thought.

McCoy finally saw the trail leading up to the mine opening where the iron carts filled with ore were pushed to a sheer drop, dumped and hauled back inside. Large wooden buildings, bone white against the darker earth, probably housed the stamping and smelting operation. A trail emerged from the ground below him. The men seemed to ride into town quite a bit.

On the mountain range to either side of the Magnus' place were the battered remains of earlier mines, their buildings toppled, quiet in their isolated solitude.

Spur urged his horse on. Following the trail, he rode between low hills that had been thrust from the desert floor in prehistoric times.

He cleared the hillocks and headed over open ground less than a mile from the mine. A rifle blasted behind him. Spur struggled to control his spooked horse, ducking and wondering who the hell was shooting at him now.

CHAPTER SEVEN

The rifle's explosion drifted away on a light desert breeze. Spur calmed his horse and slung up his Winchester, but the unseen gunmen's weapon fell silent. He must be behind one of the rocky hills.

"What are you doing out here?" a gruff voice yelled at him.

"Trying to keep my head in one piece!"

"Just a warning shot. If I'd wanted to kill you, you wouldn't be breathing now. State your business!"

An advance guard for Cleve Magnus? Sounded like it. "I'm here to see your boss. I'm with the government investigating the silver robberies. Mayor Kincaid from Oreville sent me here." And, Spur thought, hadn't told him about this little problem he might encounter.

Silence.

"Come on!" Spur said.

"Name?"

He sighed. "Spur McCoy. I sent Magnus a telegram saying I was arriving in Oreville yesterday and that I'd be out to see him."

"Okay. He tole me about you," the invisible gunman finally answered. "Now git before I change my mind!"

Spur rode on. He never saw the man.

A few minutes later her went through the whole procedure again. Warning shot. Challenge. Explanation. Hesitation. Permission to pass. Cleve Magnus wasn't taking any chances.

The mine came into sharp view as he started up the gentle slope toward it. It looked big enough to have fifty men working it. The operation was huge. Buildings were everywhere. Men streamed in and out of the mine and the large structures. A corral housed dozens of horses. Smoke rose from what must be the cookhouse. Hell, Magnus had his own blacksmith's shop.

As Spur rode into the camp, two men with rifles slung over their shoulders walked up and silently escorted McCoy to a hitching post.

"Tie her up," one of the men said, and spat a long brown stream of tobacco juice onto the sand. It sizzled.

They took him into the two-story building. Inside, it was bright and airy but the furnishings were minimal, no-nonsense. They went past a room full of tables and chairs and then up the stairs. The men deposited him before an opened door and walked away.

Spur went in. Cleve P. Magnus sat behind a plain pine desk reading a New York newspaper. He grumbled, realized that he had a visitor and stood.

For a man with that much firepower, Magnus was surprisingly short. Thin and balding, the big-jowled mine owner smiled broadly at Spur.

"Can't be too careful," he said, gruffly apologizing for his welcome. "Glad you could make it."

They shook hands.

"Have a seat, McCoy."

"Why so much protection for the mine?" Spur asked as he settled onto a hard, rail-backed chair.

Magnus fiddled with a pencil. "I'm convinced they'll try to rob me here, too. Get the goods before I can ship them anywhere. We smelt the damn stuff right here. Usual production is twenty pounds of silver a day. Yesterday, we did near to a hundred! Gave all the men a raise. As soon as news spreads in town those thieving bastards might get new ideas."

"I see."

Cleve shook his head. "All that silver ain't worth a damn if some bastard's gonna take it from me."

"Who's been robbing you? The post office? The stage coach? Who's behind all this, Magnus?"

He threw up his hands. "Damned if I know!"

"Got any enemies?"

Magnus shook his head. "Pay my men better than any other miner in Nevada." He grinned. "Shit, McCoy, I'm nice to old ladies. I only screw girls who wanna be screwed. Never touch whiskey or cards. Never stabbed a man in the back, always fight fair. I don't take what doesn't belong to me and I pump lots of money into Oreville." He shook his head. "It don't make sense!"

"Magnus, the two men who robbed your last coach shipment are dead. Found them in the desert this morning."

His eyes widened. "You sure about that? Did those two women identify them?"

"Not yet. But I did. Saw them try to murder Emma and Melissa Grieve yesterday. And they took some shots at me last night. Now they're dead."

Cleve Magnus rubbed his chin. "So it might be over? You mean I can get back to worrying about production and fights among my men and not these shitty robberies? Damn, that'd be nice!"

"Don't think so. From all appearances, the two were working for someone else. Your problems aren't over yet."

Magnus snapped the pencil. "Figures," he said, lowering his eyes. "I've never done anything to deserve this," he said. "Nothing!"

"You got lucky. Struck it rich. Some men think that's enough."

Magnus stood. "I'll be *damned* if I'm gonna let some unwashed thief take my silver!" he thundered, pounding his desk with his fist. "Damn him! Damn him!" Thump. Thwack. His lean face tightened.

"Magnus, I'm here to help you."

"Right. Sure! Can you guarantee that I won't lose another shipment? No. Shit, I don't know what to do!" Magnus walked to the window and stared out the dusty glass at his domain. "I'm putting four men inside the next eastern stage and another next to the driver. Every one of them are crack shots. *That* shipment won't be stolen unless an army attacks it."

"Yeah?"

"Yeah." He took a deep breath. "My men are spreading the word in town. That bastard'd have to be suicidal to go after the stage."

Spur nodded. "How much you shipping?"

Cleve Magnus rifled through the ink-splotched papers on his desk. "Here it is. A hundred pounds." He looked up at Spur. "You know how much pure silver I've stockpiled out here?"

McCoy shook his head.

"At least 2,000 pounds. More all the time. That's why I'm fearful that the idiot might try to get it directly from the source."

"Not likely."

"But there's a chance. There's always a chance!" Magnus yanked on his thinning hair. "It used to be so peaceful out here. Now I'm watching my back. Posting men in the desert as lookouts. Stockpiling the stuff when I should be shipping silver back east to my bank to be invested. Hell, McCoy; I'm going out of my goddamn bean!"

"Understandable, but calm down."

"Calm down?" he demanded.

"Yes. If you get any more spooked you might go crazy and shoot your own men." He had a thought. "They're loyal to you, right?"

Magnus vigorously nodded. "Damn straight! Made sure of that. Weeded out the ones who weren't. And just in case some of them get a few big ideas, I keep the silver in ten different safes scattered all over this house. There's only one entrance. No one but me knows all the combinations. It'd take a third of my men to blow them all, if they had the time, the opportunity and the dynamite." He shrugged. "No, I don't see any problems along those lines, McCoy."

"Good. Sounds like you need all the friends you

can get."

"Yeah. Why are you here, McCoy? How come the U.S. Government sent you out to this Godforsaken place?"

"The Secret Service gets its nose bent out of shape when mail is stolen, like yours was. I also understand that next month you're making a large shipment directly to the Bureau of Engraving and Printing?"

Magnus grimaced. "That's a fact. Send them silver three times a year."

Spur smiled. "My boss also wants to make sure you can supply them with the materials needed to mint U.S. coins. That's why I'm here. I can—and will—stop this man."

"Yeah?" He smirked. "I'd be greatly obliged to you if you do. But you don't mind me guarding my own goods, do you?"

Spur shook his head.

"Good."

"I have a feeling your next shipment will be safe from at least two would-be thieves."

"Hope you're right."

Spur knew it was time to leave. He stood. "Keep looking over your left shoulder. I'll be back when I know more."

"I will, and you do that."

They shook hands again.

Magnus's lookouts allowed Spur to pass unchallenged on his way from the mine. He never saw them; they were well concealed. Still, McCoy waved as he passed the general areas where he'd been confronted.

Well over an hour later he rode up to the pile of

brush where he and Kincaid had seen the bodies. They were gone, the only signs that they'd ever been there were the brick-red stains on the sand. The mayor had cheated the buzzards out of supper that day.

He took a few swallows of water and offered some to his mare, who gratefully drank. As he stood in the wash, resting, getting his bearings, he heard a rider approach.

Spur covered the horse's wet muzzle with a hand to quiet her and led her into the deepest part of the wash. He stood motionless, watching the line of dust that marked the rider's passage speed from left to right over the ridge.

When it had fully passed Spur turned and looked. The man had to be going to the mine. Spur decided to wait. He found some jerky in a saddlebag and had a frugal lunch, slowly chewing the hard food. His horse found a scrubby bush and had its meal.

Afterward, Spur climbed a low ridge, shifted the brim of his hat to shade his eyes, and searched the landcape. The tiny figure of a rider moved in the distance directly toward Cleve Magnus's mine. He soon lost sight of it.

Spur took off his shirt and splashed some water onto his chest. He waited, drawing maps of the mine in the sand with a short stick. Taking the role of the thief, he imagined how he'd try to attack the mine itself.

Magnus's operation was guarded on one side by sheer walls of solid rock. They were impossible to climb. Only a frontal or side approach was possible. Maybe all three. He stared at the sketchy map, wondering if the desert sun had finally gotten to him.

Another hour passed. McCoy sat on the dirt and
jabbed a stick at a furious scorpion, who lifted its
tail and ran in circles to warn its attacker of an
impending sting. He was soon bored and threw the
stick at the scorpion. Unharmed, it trotted to a
nearby rock and disappeared.

Spur bided his time.

In her office at the Motherlode Saloon, Julie
Golden re-read the telegram that she'd received that
morning. It was clear. She hadn't misunderstood
the message that Lionel Kemp had hidden in the
words. He'd decided to go ahead and have her do it.

She thought of the new man she'd met, a
foreigner that her male employees said could be
trusted. Julie had wasted no time after receiving
Lionel's telegram in putting his plan into action.
She wasn't merely satisfying his whim. The woman
saw a shining possibility in his latest scheme.

A direct assault on the mine. Take the silver
directly from it. No more grabbing a measly few
pounds here and there.

A war.

She sighed, folded the telegram and stuffed it into
the drawer where she kept the receipts of the girl's
wages. If only this man worked out, Julie thought.
If only he did what he was supposed to do and they
were successful in their mission. If only Lionel
Kemp didn't arrive back in Oreville until
afterward. If only . . . .

She shook her head. "Julie Golden, stop thinking
about it," she said out loud. The businesswoman
cleared her desk, brushed off the ashes that one of

her customers had unceremoniously dumped into its teak surface and straightened her hair.

She'd already talked to Burt, Harris and Pete about the possibility of finding several dozen gunmen. Her friends had been encouraging. All she was waiting for was—what was his name? Julie smiled at the memory of how her bartender had pointed him out to her downstairs.

She'd dragged him to her office. Once there, they'd talked and made love at the same time. He was uncertain but agreed to have a look at the place.

He was quite a man, she thought. She hoped Phillipas Telonia had good news on his arrival.

Julie sighed and pushed back her chair. Time to leave. He was to meet her at her house.

The rider finally returned. Spur got a glimpse of his face—dark and bearded. Whoever he was, he'd ridden out to Cleve Magnus's operation, hadn't been challenged and had left almost as soon as he'd arrived.

He probably didn't work there. Maybe he'd gone to survey the lay of the land. If he knew about the outposts he could circle away from them and still get a good look.

Spur shrugged. Maybe Magus was right. Perhaps the man behind the robberies was planning to hit the mine itself. But when?

And how?

CHAPTER EIGHT

" 'Bout time you got back here!" Julie Golden said as the tall, bearded man brushed past her and walked into the kitchen. She closed and locked the door. "What'd you see at the mine?"

"Nothing good." The immigrant brushed caked dust from his coat and strode toward the bottle of whiskey that Julie kept on a shelf. Staring at the wall, he took a swallow.

"Phil! Phillipas!" Julie said, running to him. "Well?"

The frowning Greek wiped his lips. "Well what?"

She smiled. "Okay, you're tired. I understand. I'll have plenty of hot water for your bath in a few minutes."

He grunted. "Julie, we cannot do it."

"Why not?" she demanded.

Phillipas Telonia sighed and sat in a chair, staring down at the huge metal bathtub. "Perhaps if we had eighty men, maybe. But otherwise—"

"Don't talk," Julie said, shaking her head. "A lot of men can't think straight right after a hard ride. I know I can't," she quipped.

"No, no. It is not that." Phillipas shook his head again. "The mine, it is like a fortress. Guards everywhere. Magnus must have twenty or thirty men out there." He stroked the tips of his thick, black moustache. "Even with surprise on our side, we would need at least as many, maybe even forty men. Forty men might be enough."

"Don't talk." Julie smiled and walked to the stove, lifted the big copper pot and poured the last of the hot water into the tub. "You take off your clothes and get into that dang thing! I'll make you something to eat."

"Julie. Julie, look at me!" he demanded.

She did. He still took her breath away.

"I will not ride out to certain death for anyone. There is no way that you can do this."

"But—"

"No."

She sighed. So that was that. Or was it? "Here, let me help you undress." Julie knelt before him and took the booted foot that he stuck out toward her. She tugged. "Nothing's impossible, Phillipas. You got out of Greece before they caught you." Julie grimaced and pulled. "Now you're here just when I need you." The boot started to slip. "And together, there's nothing we can't do!"

"Except take off my boots?"

Julie smiled and yanked as hard as she could. It slid from his foot. "See? Nothing to it."

"Maybe." Phillipas flashed her a smile. "But

Julie, you cannot hire that many men."

"Why not?" The second boot easily came off. "There's plenty of them in this town who'd do it."

"You cannot trust them."

"Can't I?" Julie rose to her feet. "Phillipas, the men of Oreville haven't worked for months. They're desperate for money, even just to scrape up enough to leave. I'll find as many as you say we need."

He ripped off his woolen socks and scratched his left foot.

"But enough about that for now. Stand up, you big oaf!"

Phil grunted. "Feta cheese. I want some feta cheese!" He slammed a fist onto the table.

"There's no feta cheese in my kitchen. And you aren't eating until you get your bath!" She waved the air in front of her nose. "You need it."

"Okay, okay. But no food after. Just you and me." He ripped off his shirt and hauled down his pants.

"No underdrawers again, Phil?" Julie said, shaking her head as the naked man stepped into the tub.

"Too hot here."

Julie knelt beside him, dipped water in her hands and poured it over his head. The Greek spluttered.

"We can do it. I've done some checking. Three of my best employees say they can get all the men we need. Good shots, reliable, trustworthy."

He turned to her.

"Don't be surprised, Phillipas. This is my last chance of ever leaving Oreville and that—that *man* I told you about this morning. We can do it together." Julie picked up the cake of lye soap and a rough cloth. "Can't we?"

He sighed as she scrubbed his broad back. "You speak of war, my lady. War!"

She rubbed harder and bent her mouth to his ear. "Yes, General Telonia."

Spur McCoy's horse was foaming by the time he rode into Oreville. He tied the beast's reins to the hitching post, gave her a quick rub down and entered the Eastern Heights Hotel.

"Emma and Melissa in?" he asked the manager, who bent over the ledger.

"Huh? What?"

"The two women who were involved in the stage-coach robbery. You seen them?"

"Naw. Not since they walked out last night. Ain't been back, that's fer sure. Leastwise, not that Melissa. I'd remember her," the balding man said, and scratched his chin. "Ain't she a looker?"

"Yeah." He went to the stairs.

When Spur's urgent knock roused no one inside the womens' room, he opened the door with a skeleton key and went in. There were no signs of a struggle. Except for the shot-out wall, nothing looked unusual. Clothing had been placed in neat piles. The younger woman's underthings were laid out on the bed, ready to be worn. But the women weren't there.

The smell of Melissa's perfume hung in the air. Where were they?"

Spur went next door and knocked. A bleary-eyed, red-nosed cowboy nearly fell onto him as he opened the door. McCoy backed away from the liquor-laced breath.

"You know where the two women in the room next to yours went?"

The cowboy reeled, gripped the door frames and belched. "You got a dollar? I drunk up all my money and—and—"

Spur shrugged, retrieved a silver dollar from his pocket and held it out.

"Thanks, stranger. Sure. Melissa and that old bag headed out after supper last night."

"Where?"

He snatched the money and stormed past the Secret Service agent. "To Ma's. I saw 'em myself. Now I got me somethin' important to do."

Ma's? The woman who had the ugliest girls in town? The one the barber had told him about as he chopped off his hair? Spur watched the cowboy go, closed both doors and went down the stairs.

A woman like Emma Grieve didn't seem the type of lady who'd go into a saloon, but it was worth checking. The drunkard's thirst might have led him to say anything. Still, there were only two saloons in town that were still open after the boom years. He might as well visit them both.

Neither was named Ma's.

Stale smoke stung his eyes in the Placer, a dark, dusty, fly-buzzing saloon. The apron dozed, his left cheek plastered to the sticky bar. The stairs that led to the upper floor had been boarded up. One solitary drinker sat back in his chair, clutching a half-empty bottle with jealous hands.

Spur walked to the bartender and thumped his shoulder. The man stirred and opened his eyes.

"Yuh?"

"Is Ma here?"

"Hell no! And don't mention her. That hussy's stolen all my customers!"

Spur turned to leave as the apron's cheek hit the bar again.

Grunting, he walked across the street and down one block to the Motherlode. Inside, kerosene lamps shone. The floor was freshly swept. A huge mirror over the bar doubled the apparent size of the large, well-kept saloon. The bar itself was an oak and brass monstrosity, obviously brought there at great cost from back east.

This must be Ma's place, he thought. It had a softer edge than what most drinking men demanded. Green velvet curtains were bunched at the corners of the windows. The brass spittoons shone with regular polishing. Even the bartender looked as if he'd just been pressed with a sad iron.

Twenty men had assembled there to satisfy their guts and their groins. They drank and gambled, filling the air with curses and shouts and wild whoops as a plain-faced girl trudged down the stairs. Some of them must be Magnus's workers.

Two other girls worked the saloon. Spur watched them and ordered a whiskey. They weren't ugly, but certainly were nothing to write home about. Maybe the barber hadn't been as kind to them as he could have been.

"Damn her!"

Spur glanced to the left of him at the bar. The woman who'd just emerged from upstairs tugged at the bodice of her dress, readjusting her breasts. "Damn her to hell! That hussy thinks she can take

all my men. Ha! Let me tell you something, mister;
she won't last a week!"

"Something wrong, miss?"

The green-eyed wench laughed. "No. I mean yeah.
But don't worry about it, sweetie." She patted
Spur's butt. "Nothing I can't handle. My name's
Squirrel Sue."

"McCoy."

The round-faced woman eyed him. "You're not
here for a roll, are you? I can always tell."

"No. Truth is, I'm looking for Ma."

The whore rolled her eyes and sauntered off.

Just then an auburn haired young woman,
conservatively dressed in a high necked gown of
white silk, pushed through the batwing doors,
glanced sternly at the bartender and rustled up the
stairs.

Ma, Spur wondered? She certainly didn't fit the
name, but the woman didn't look like a saloon girl
and she definitely acted as if she owned the place.

As the woman hurried up, a sullen faced man
stood at attention at the foot of the stairs, a rifle
over his shoulder.

A guard?

Spur studied the saloon. The slick bartender was
armed. He had pistols strapped to both legs. A rifle
sat beside the huge cash register. McCoy easily
spotted a second hired gunman. He casually stood
beside the entrance to the saloon, constantly eyeing
the crowd.

Why so much protection here, Spur wondered?
He sighed and sipped the watered whiskey,
thinking. Maybe Ma was a stickler for running a

clean place. But then, how many female saloon owners were there?

Muffled screams echoed from the second floor. He'd heard the like a hundred times before. Some guy gets too excited with a poor working girl and she puts up a fight. It was a sad part of the business.

Hearing the screams, the guard next to the stairs stiffened and swung the rifle into his hands. A young, blonde girl stumbled down the stairs, dressed only in her chemise and petticoats. Her makeup plastered face cringed. She desperately hurried down the narrow steps.

"The show's startin' early, boys!" one man yelled.

A buck-naked man appeared from upstairs, hopped after her and easily caught the frightened young woman.

"Come on, honey! Goddamn! I paid fer you and you's gonna get it!"

"No!"

They wrestled. The guard broke it up, forced the girl's hands behind her back and marched her to the second floor while the saloon exploded with laughter at the unexpected scene.

The cowboy, suddenly aware of the man staring at him, smiled, waved and took the stairs three at a time to recapture his unwilling prize.

Spur heard a door slam. The guard took up his post again, cool but grinning. A piano creaked into off-key life under the bony fingers of a vested player.

"I have three aces!" someone yelled. A card player across the saloon overturned a table and drew his weapon.

"Damn you, Jackson! I have two, and I ain't the one who's cheating!"

"No fighting!" the bartender shouted.

As the gamblers faced off and the piano music droned on, Spur realized that he recognized the half-dressed blonde girl who'd run down the stairs.

It was Melissa, the witness to the stagecoach robbery.

CHAPTER NINE

"You foolish girl!" Julie Golden stared at the cowering young woman. "Don't you want to get out of Oreville? Don't you want to see Philadelphia again, to get away from these robberies and guns?"

"And men?" Emma Grieve yelled over the saloon owner's shoulder.

Melissa hugged her shoulders and backed into the corner of her room. She raised her knees, unconsciously protecting the most private part of her body. The part that they wanted her to use. Tears ran down her cheeks. She shook. "How can you do this to me, grandmother?"

"It's all for the best, my dear," Emma Grieve reached out a hand but quickly retracted it. "It's the only way I can see that we'll ever leave this hell-hole. You know I don't have any savings. We're broke, Melissa." She softened her face. "Trust me, darling. It isn't so bad. I had some good times! Flat on my back, making money, meeting all sorts of interesting gentlemen. It was *fun!*"

Melissa sucked in her breath. "Grandmother!"

"Listen to her, child." Julie Golden smiled. "And wise up. You insulted my customer by running out of your room like that. I'll have to give him his money back and still send him to my best girl all because of you." Julie turned to the elderly woman. "Talk some sense into her, Emma. Will you?"

She set her lined face. "I'll try. Melissa, you're no virgin."

The girl turned from her.

"I know all about your shenanigans with the Miller boys, with Ted Pollard and David Seaton and—"

Melissa sighed and cut off her words. "Alright! What are you trying to say?"

Emma smiled. "At any rate, you're been with more than a few boys. And you're no more of a Christian woman than I am. That's why I don't understand you, girl. This nice lady's offering to pay you to do what you'd normally do for free! Why, if I was any younger and prettier, I might have a go at it myself."

Melissa lifted her head. "I like to chose my men. Besides, he smelled bad. And he wanted to do something to me that was so disgusting."

Julie hooted. "Hell, nothing's disgusting if they pay right. And he did. Ten dollars! You and Emma would've gotten half. Look what you've done!" She threw up her hands.

"I don't care. I'm leaving." Melissa rose and grabbed the dress that lay on the small bed.

"No you're not, young woman!" Julie advanced

on her. "You and your grandmother are staying here for your own protection. You can't be on the streets. It's not safe. And look what happened in your hotel room! Those robbers are still looking for you. So earn some money. I'll have some men escort you to the stagecoach when it's time. If you see ten men a day—"

"*Ten men!*" she shrieked.

"—you'll be out of here in no time." Julie went to the girl and took the dress from her hands. "There, there, Melissa. It's the only way. Your grandmother knows it, and so do you. Quit whining. Make yourself pretty. Get ready for your next customer. Okay?"

Melissa turned to her grandmother, but Emma Grieve crossed her bony arms and turned her face to the ceiling. The girl plopped onto the bed and brushed back her hair. She tried an unconvincing smile.

"What—what am I supposed to do?" Melissa asked her temporary employer.

"Don't worry. They'll tell you exactly what they want. One week," Julie Golden said. "In one week your troubles will be over."

She left the room and closed the door behind her. In the hall, Julie took a deep breath and straightened her back. That idiotic girl! Lionel Kemp would have Melissa and Emma killed if he heard they were still alive when he came back into town. But there was no way to tell them that.

She sighed and returned to her office. She had a business to run.

"I'm Alice. You want me?" She smiled, showing

a set of bad teeth, and pulled up a chair at Spur's table. The whore took a healthy swallow from his watered whiskey.

He thought it over. It would be difficult to get past the guard stationed at the stairs without causing a commotion. The girl was his ticket up there.

Spur McCoy looked her over. "You'll do."

Alice laughed and stood. "Honey, I'll do everything!"

She took his arm and dragged him to the stairs. The guard didn't look at the couple as they walked to the second floor. She turned to him once they'd reached the landing.

"The room at the end of the hall," she said, her face flushed at the prospect of money. "Tell Ma you're seeing Alice, her best girl. You pay her."

"Okay."

"A yellow feather means nothing special. Any other color means specialties, and I do 'em all!"

"Fine." Spur went to the door and knocked.

"Come in, sir."

Spur walked in, hat in his hand. The room smelled of roses. Jars of feathers littered the small desk. Behind it sat the young, attractive woman he'd seen striding into the Motherlode Saloon. Ma.

"What can I do for you?" Julie Golden set down her quill and smiled up at him.

"I guess Alice. Nothing special."

Julie smirked. "Fine. Five dollars."

"Ah, isn't that a little much?"

Julie jerked back in false indignation. "For my beautiful girls? No. Besides, that includes the free show that starts in two minutes."

Show? Spur finally remembered what the barber had told him just after he arrived in town. "Okay."

He placed a much folded fiver on Ma's desk.

"Let me make a note of this."

Spur thought as she bent over the ledger. She's a businesswoman all right, but he couldn't believe that Julie Golden was somehow connected with the silver robberies.

But he had seen Melissa in her saloon. And Melissa had been in the middle of one of the hold-ups.

"The show's in room 2. Be there on time, sir." She handed him a yellow plume. "This'll get you into it and into Alice's room right after."

He stalled. This was going much too fast. "I really didn't want Alice."

Ma lifted her eyebrows. "No?"

"No. What about that blonde girl I saw earlier?"

She shrugged. "Honey, half of them's blonde! Which one are you talking about? She might be busy now, but you could always wait."

Spur smoothed on a smile. "A wild one who ran down the stairs in her underthings a minute back."

Julie Golden smiled. "Heck, that's the new girl. She can't do anything—yet. I have to break her in. Come back in a week. She'll be ready for you then. Now git!"

"Yes, ma'am."

Spur smirked at her and walked out. He found Alice hurrying into room two, grabbed her arm and handed her the feather.

"Go right in and watch the show, but keep the damned thing or we'll both get into trouble. I have to get ready."

Drunken men brushed past him into the small room.

"I changed my mind. See you around."

"What? Come back here, stranger! Shit, you're the best lookin' man I've seen in years!"

McCoy laughed as he went down the stairs.

So Melissa was the new girl. She might be there by choice, but it sure hadn't looked like it. Julie Golden must be forcing her into working. But why?

Spur had to get her. And he couldn't do it alone. He needed help.

Mayor Kincaid wasn't in his office, but an adenoidal deputy said that he'd just gone to the telegraph office. Spur hurried there.

As he walked into the rickety building he saw Mayor Kincaid standing with his back to the door. The harried telegraph operator grabbed a pen.

"Just a second, mayor. Just a second! The sender has to repeat this message. I missed it the first time." He threw him an angry look.

"Alright. No problem," Kincaid said.

Standing in the door, Spur heard the familiar clack of the machine. He remembered when he'd posed as a telegraph man on an assignment years ago. He'd had to master Morse code. Did he still remember it?

The message began. Spur was surprised to find he could decode it as it came in over the wire:

"Oreville, Nevada
Julie. STOP. Had to halt here, STOP.

Silver-haired lady smiles at me, STOP.
Say she'll be mine tomorrow, STOP.
Lionel."

Spur puzzled over the strange message as the
machine fell silent. He memorized it. Was it in
code? Could be. But who was Julie?

"Okay, Boyd. I've waited long enough!" Kincaid
said.

Another message started clicking into the room.

"Fer chrissakes! Never mind. I'll come back!" The
mayor turned toward the door. "McCoy!"

"I was just coming to see you, mayor."

They walked outside.

"Ah, who's Julie?"

"Who's Julie? Just the owner of the best saloon
in town. The Motherlode. Her name's Julie Golden,
but everyone calls her Ma."

"Thanks."

"Have to be running." He turned to go.

"Wait, Kincaid!"

"Sorry, Duty calls. I've got to get to that damned
church social, if you'll pardon the expression,"
Kincaid said.

Spur grabbed the back of his coat. "We have to
talk!"

"Not now. See you about half-past." The mayor
bolted down the street toward the distant chapel.

As the mayor trotted off, Spur thought. Someone
had sent the telegram to Julie, to Ma. The message
was so strange that he went over it again and again.
Following an ingrained habit, he tossed out the
unimportant words. Everything seemed to fall into

place.

It was in code. He'd sent enough messages like it that he could spot one.

Silver-haired lady. *Mine. Tomorrow.*

The real message could read:

> "Oreville, Nevada
> Julie, STOP. Had to halt here, STOP.
> Silver mine tomorrow, STOP.
> Lionel."

Spur's face flushed. It seemed right. It felt right. A man named Lionel was letting Julie know that something was happening at the silver mine tomorrow.

But what? McCoy tried to convince himself that the hardened saloon keeper was involved in the silver robberies. The telegram almost convinced him.

Julie Golden had Melissa. The girl could be in danger, especially if this Julie was what he thought she was.

He stood. McCoy had to get her out of there.

CHAPTER TEN

Phillipas Telonia passed Spur McCoy as he raced for the batwing doors. The Greek sidled up to the bar and raised a finger. Pete, the bartender, slapped a glass of whiskey in front of him.

"No ouzo?" he said, grunting.

Pete grinned. "Christ, you know what we have by now. Been hanging around here ever since you got into town." The clean-shaven bartender leaned toward him. "I told you when you hit Oreville to leave. There hasn't been any mining around here for months! Unless you call working for that Magnus mining!" He sent a circular wad of spit flying into the brass spittoon behind the bar.

"I know." Phillipas shifted the glass back and forth, staring into the amber liquid that it contained.

"Say, Telonia," Pete said. He lowered his voice. "What's with Ma? She's acting mighty peculiar."

He grunted.

"Bringing that new girl here. Leaving for home all the time and putting me in charge of her office!" He flared his nostrils. "Now she wants me to round up all these men who're handy with rifles. What is she up to?"

The Greek was silent.

"Hell, you can tell me!" Pete broadly smiled. "I'm her best employee. Worked for her since she bought the place. Never given her no trouble." The apron's voice dropped to a whisper. "Is she planning something big?"

Phillipas Telonia grinned. "Yes."

As he took a slow sip of the strange drink, he sighed and thought about Athens. His sweetheart who'd left him for the baker's son. His parents' graves overlooking the sea. The stone house where he used to live.

Then it had happened. He'd drunk too much ouzo, listened to too much Bouzouki music, smashed too many plates. The dancing, the dark-haired women, the heat of the Mediterranean night had gotten to him.

He hadn't planned to break the bottle and toss it into the air. He didn't aim, or tried to plant the jagged glass through the strange man's skull. But it had happened.

Phillipas remembered how he'd walked out, hired onto a fishing boat and ran from one port to another, from country to country, just a day ahead of the Greek police.

The mayor hadn't liked watching his father die that night.

And now, this goddess of a woman offered him

money to wage a personal war. It was hopeless, but he saw something in her eyes that reminded him of home.

So he'd do it. Phillipas drained the glass.

"So whiskey ain't too bad after all, is it?" Pete asked him.

What would happen at the mine? An attack? Impossible, Spur thought as he strode down Main Street. No woman could muster the number of men necessary to launch a successful assault on such a well guarded place. She didn't have the military experience to carry it off. Still, someone named Lionel had sent her the telegram. If he was behind all this, and it seemed that he was, he could hire the men for her.

Spur snarled and ran. He caught up with the mayor thirty feet from the church. "Kincaid, I don't care how many old ladies are waiting for you in there. We have to talk!"

The mayor shook his head. "You again, McCoy? If I don't show for the church social those fine ladies'll make damned sure I don't get reelected."

"Kincaid!" he bellowed. Spur felt the veins pop out on his forehead.

"Okay, okay. Jesus! What is it?"

"Know anyone named Lionel?"

The mayor scratched his chin. "Lionel. Sure! Lionel Stander farms dust on the trail heading west." Kincaid shrugged. "And there's Lionel Dreeson, Paul and Mary's son. Lionel Atwater, Lionel Curtis—"

"Okay. Okay!" Spur sighed. "Mayor, I need some help. Have to bust someone out of Ma's place."

The mayor threw back his head and laughed. "Hell, McCoy! Getting all moral on me or something? It'd take more manpower than we have in the whole town to force the men who go in there to leave against their will. Or most of the girls, for that matter."

"Not that! Kincaid, remember the women who were on the stage when it was robbed of Magnus's silver? The young girl and her grandmother?"

"Sure, Melissa and Emma Grieve. Why?"

"I just saw the girl in the Motherlode. Looked to me like she's being held there, forced into working for Ma."

"So?" He sniffed.

"Kincaid, we gotta get her out of there."

"Why? Stop talking nonsense, McCoy!" He spat. The thick saliva sizzled on the street. "Ma's no slave driver. Any of her girls could walk out of there whenever she wanted to. You've been drinking too much."

"I have some information that seems to link Julie Golden with the silver robberies."

The mayor whistled.

"Ma's hired extra security in her saloon—a guard at the stairs and one at the door. I don't know what all this is leading to, but we've got to get the girl to safety."

"Okay, okay, McCoy. Maybe you're right. But you've gotta help me explain to the church ladies after we clean up this mess."

"Forget about them! Come on. You can get me upstairs without causing too much trouble, right?"

"Well . . . ."

"Don't you know Julie Golden?"

"Sure. Yeah I know her!" he thundered. "And I'm not ashamed to say it!"

"Let's see her. Now!"

"You're some woman, Emma Grieve," Julie Golden said to the woman seated across her desk. "I never would have suspected that you used to earn an honest living like that."

Emma cracked a smile and crossed her legs. "I was young. It was fun and I made some money. That's why I can't understand why Melissa isn't taking to this." She shook her head, ruffling the black lace that fringed her bonnet. "The girl's lacking in plain sense, she is."

Ma's laughter filled her office. "I'm sure she'll do fine, Emma. After she gets used to it. They all do, you know. All the girls who came out west to be singers or dancers and ended up under my roof. Oh, they may fight it at first, but in the end they just lie back and let the men do what they want."

Emma set her gaze on the attractive young woman. "Julie, why are you doing this? What's in it for you?"

"What do you think? Money! Melissa is beautiful, young and inexperienced. Your granddaughter will be a welcome change for my steady customers. Some of these men have had every one of my girls ten times. She's just what I needed."

"I see." Emma lowered her eyes. "We're beholden to you, Julie. Me and Melissa. If she starts acting up again I'll—I'll whip her into doing it!"

"I'm sure that won't be necessary. She'll come around. And before you know it, I'll be seeing you off on the eastbound stage."

"That will be a fine day!" Emma rose on steady feet. "I should get some rest, I guess."

"Alright. Don't worry about Melissa, Emma."

"I'll try not to."

As the wizened old woman tottered from her office, Julie sighed and sank into her cushioned chair. It was necessary to keep the women there. Even though Lionel was out of town, he had plenty of men in Oreville who would shoot Melissa and Emma on sight if they'd been ordered to do so.

Julie hoped that he wouldn't return until after the stage had carted the Grieves from Oreville, far from the danger that lay all around them.

Ever the businesswoman, Julie brightened as the door opened.

"What are you doing in here, you little brat? You're twelve if you're a day old. Scram and come back in ten years!

"Telegram, Miss Golden." The freckled-faced boy awkwardly held out a folded piece of paper.

"Oh, sorry. Buy yourself a soda." Julie exchanged the note for a quarter and spread it on her desk.

Lionel's message pleased her. He'd given her the okay. She would attack the mine.

Drunken cardplayers shouted greetings to Kincaid as McCoy followed the mayor into the Motherlode Saloon. They casually walked through the boisterous bar. Justin Kincaid stopped at the foot of the stairs.

"Gotta see Ma about business, Harris," he said.

The guard grunted. "Go ahead. But your friend—"

"Goes with me! Come on!"

The politician who'd been cowed by a few old ladies vigorously strode up the stairs. McCoy was relieved to see the change of character.

They stopped on the landing. "Which room?" Spur asked in a whisper.

"I dunno. Alice is in 4, Marsha's in 3." As he rattled off the numbers and their occupants, the mayor's face brightened at the attendant memories. "Ah, let's see. As far as I know rooms 13 and 14 are empty. The two girls who used to live in them left town last month."

They walked down the hall. The liquid sounds of flesh banging together emanated from the rooms. The smell of perfume and sweat permeated the air. Ma's was busy, Spur thought as he stood before room 13.

"My lucky number," he said. McCoy glanced sharply at Kincaid. They both drew their weapons.

He opened the door. Melissa Grieve stared up at them in unconcealed horror. The girl's hair was mussed. Her bodice and petticoats were torn to ribbons.

"You can't make me stay here!" she hissed. "I know you work for Ma!"

"Quiet, girl!" Spur said. "We're here to help you." He threw her a blanket. "Wrap this around yourself!"

"Why?" she demanded.

"Just do it, Melissa!"

"McCoy, distract them!" The mayor jerked his head toward the hall.

"Right."

He holstered his weapon and quietly ran down the stairs. The guard stared up at him.

"Come quick," he said with feigned urgency. "And get the other guy! Ma wants you *now*!"

The muscular tough stood and turned his head toward the saloon's front door. "Burt, get yer ass upstairs!" he yelled.

Spur made it up in time to surprise Harris. He slammed the butt of his revolver into the guard's skull, digging it into the hard flesh and bone. Another sharp blow broke the skin. Harris grunted, spasmed and dropped.

Burt bounded up the stairs. Spur stepped out of sight.

"What the hell! You drunk or something, Harris? Get off yer fat butt!"

The guard bent over his downed friend. Mayor Kincaid and a blanket-wrapped Melisssa emerged from room 13.

"Hey!"

Spur cut off the man's word with a well-placed kick and a smashing blow to his head. Burt crumpled on top of Harris.

"Come on!" McCoy yelled to Kincaid.

The three of them hurried down the stairs. Spur surveyed the scene as they descended into the saloon. A few men who'd noticed the altercation looked up and went back to the business of serious drinking and poker.

"Hey!" a lean cowboy shouted, staring at the trio. "They're taking away the new girl!"

Spur found his group the center of attention. He firmed his grip on Melissa's arms.

"Stay out of my way, George!" the mayor yelled to a friend.

They slid between the scattered tables and chairs

toward the distant door. McCoy urged Justin Kincaid to move faster.

A sudden thought ripped through him. The bartender!

Spur crashed through two sodden men. He and Kincaid rushed toward the door, fighting through the snarl of angry drunks bent on keeping the new girl at their disposal. Fists flew. He took a solid punch on his chin.

"Damnit, people! This is serious!" the mayor yelled. "Get out of our way!"

"Like hell they will!"

Spur saw a knife slicing through the air toward them.

CHAPTER ELEVEN

The deadly knife dug into the saloon wall inches from Spur's head, splintering the wood with a loud crack. A rifle blasted into life.

Melissa screamed and went limp in the two men's hands. Spur grimaced at Kincaid.

"You ain't leaving with that girl," the bartender yelled. He walked toward them, his eye to his rifle's sight. "Let her go and get the hell out of my saloon!"

Spur straightened his back. There were other ways to get out of a tight spot than firing. "What's wrong with you? You want this poor girl to bleed to death right here?"

"What?" The fancily dressed bartender squinted through his rifle sight.

Kincaid caught on. "That's right, Pete! Some bastard beat her up pretty bad. Me and McCoy here had just left Ma's office when we saw him. He knocked out Harris and Burt. Before we could stop him he jumped out the window!"

"You don't want this girl's death on your hands, do you?" Spur said. Melissa wavered on her feet, but McCoy knew she wasn't acting. She was overwhelmed by what was happening.

"Well—well—" the apron stammered.

Spur took a step toward the door behind him. "Lower your weapon, Pete. We're taking her out of here."

"Do it!" the mayor thundered.

The bartender's aim faltered. "But shit, Mayor Kincaid! Ma's told me to—"

"What's Ma told you to do?"

He froze at the woman's words. Pete lowered his rifle and wearily turned to face his employer. Julie Golden cleared the stairs, put her hands on her pretty hips and walked up to her employee.

Spur admired her coolness, the way she tilted her chin. The woman was in total control.

"Sam, if the girl's been injured she should be looked after. Isn't that right? What kind of a person do you think I am?" Julie shook her head.

The bartender gaped. "But, Ma!"

She brushed past him and fixed her gaze on Spur's. She smiled. "Go ahead. Take her. Quickly!"

"Thanks a lot, Ma. I'll pay double next time," the mayor said.

The two men helped Melissa through the batwing doors. Once they were in the sunlight she straightened up, fresh as can be.

"Who *are* you people?" the girl asked, looking from one to the other.

"No time for that now. Kincaid, where's the safest place to drop her?"

He snapped his fingers. "Post office! It's guarded day and night."

"Fine."

"Wait!" Melissa stepped toward the doors. "My grandmother's still in there!"

"In the saloon?"

She vigorously nodded, flinging yellow hair around her head. "We can't leave her in there with that woman!"

Emma Grieve burst through the batwings. "Land sakes, child! What's happened?"

Spur snorted. "No time to explain, granny. We're taking you somewhere safe."

"From whom?" she demanded. "We have to get Melissa to a doctor!"

"She's fine."

"I am, grandmother. Really!" The girl smiled and grabbed the elderly woman's hand.

Kincaid and McCoy escorted the pair to the post office. Spur kept an eye on the rear but no one followed them. Ma must have changed her plans.

"You were being kept there against your will, right?" he asked the suddenly vivacious girl.

"Yes! That horrid woman forced me to do the most disgusting things!"

"No, dear," Emma said. "She was helping us!"

Melissa wrung her hand from her grandmother's. "She was not!"

Incapable of figuring it out, Spur sighed and ushered them into the post office.

"We're just closing," the armed guard said as the mayor stepped in.

"Fine. These two women are in danger. Protect them around the clock with your very lives!"

"Yes, sir!" The ex-soldier braced.

"I don't understand!" Emma said as McCoy and Kincaid walked back to the door. "Why are you doing this? Miss Golden was helping us to leave Oreville!"

"I'm not sure. I don't know!" Spur threw up his hands. "It's possible that Ma's involved in the silver robberies, like the one that happened to that stage you were taking? Those might have been her men shooting at you in your hotel room."

Emma shivered. "I don't believe you," she yelled. "That' woman's a saint!"

"Maybe. Or maybe she wanted to make you both saints." Spur sighed.

"You can trust him, ladies!" Kincaid said. "Spur McCoy's a government agent. He's been sent down here to find the men who've been stealing the silver!"

"I'm not going to make you stay, Melissa," McCoy said to the girl as she fiddled with a stack of envelopes. "You're free to come and go as you like. But if you step past that door I can't be responsible for your safety. Understand?"

She nodded. "Yes. Perfectly. And I'll see to it that grandmother stays here too."

He kissed her forehead.

"Well!" Emma Grieve said.

The men walked out.

"They'll be safe enough there," Kincaid said. "I'll have food and water sent into them, and the guards'll keep them company."

Spur took off his hat and slicked the wet hair from his neck. "When's the next stagecoach headed east?"

"Not until next week."

"Great. Then we'll have to find somewhere else to put them. It's been an interesting day, mayor." He sighed. "What do you think about this assault on Cleve Magnus's mine?"

"I don't know. I don't see it happening." Kincaid thoughtfully scratched his chin. "Get a good night's sleep, McCoy." He peered at him. "Looks like you could use it."

"Okay."

Spur walked to the Eastern Heights Hotel, his mind a blur of thoughts and unanswered questions.

Lionel Kemp slammed a fist into his thigh as he rode the gelding through the gathering dusk. He'd been a fool to think that Julie could handle the whole thing herself. It wasn't wise to trust a mere woman to oversee such an important mission.

So he'd changed his plans, sent her a telegram, hired a horse and started back toward Oreville. No sense in warning the bitch of his return, Kemp thought.

The sky deepened into a blue that quickly faded to black. Stars poked from the sky above his bobbing head. Lionel Kemp sighed at the forgotten feeling of a saddle under him and the world stretching out before his eyes.

It had been a long time since he'd been on the range, trying to earn a few bucks by rustling cattle. That had been so successful that he'd saved enough money to go into business in Oreville.

Back then, money was just starting to pour into the town. The mines were hitting such rich veins that he'd bought up virtually all the surrounding property. Kemp quickly quadrupled his money by selling off lots to the merchants who set up shop, hoping to cash in on the miner's luck.

Nothing held him back. Though he never staked a claim, lifted a pick axe or bought a mine, Lionel Kemp was soon the richest man in town. He saw to it that his hand-picked politicians got elected. Dozens of pretty women lined up to share his bed for the night. He owned half the men in town. The law couldn't touch him, no matter what he did. He owned that, too.

He'd lived a high life for over a year, opening his own saloons and equipment stores to soak money from the pockets of the rich men who settled in Oreville. His bank accounts swelled.

Then the nightmare had begun. The gold and silver crazed miners exhausted the earth's riches. Huge operations shut down overnight. Hundreds of people pulled up their stakes and left town. Within a week, word had spread across the country, halting the flow of fresh manpower into Oreville. Two weeks after that it was a virtual ghost town. His once valuable property wasn't worth two bits.

Lionel had gotten by. He'd lived off his earnings for as long as he could. When he'd squeezed his assets as far as they'd go, Kemp realized that he was in trouble. Unwilling to give up his comfortable lifestyle, he'd sold his last successful business—the Motherlode saloon—and looked around for something else to do.

Then it came to him. One night he woke with the perfect plan. The victim? The wealthy widow who'd bought his saloon.

Julie Golden had been easy to fool. He'd hired a savage man to kill an eighteen year old boy by bashing in his skull for $5. While the murder was happening, Kemp was busy at the woman's house, getting her falling-down drunk and taking her to bed.

After the gunman had dragged the body into her house downstairs, Kemp knocked her out and deposited the unconscious woman besides the dead boy. An empty wine bottle in her hand completed the scene. Kemp went home to let Julie come to her own conclusions.

Now that he had something on her, Lionel hatched his scheme of stealing Magnus's silver. It wasn't a good living but it was better than nothing. Then the bastard had gotten too careful, guarding his shipments. And Kemp was dangerously low on money, no more than two month's worth. He had to clean out the mine of its stored riches and head out of town forever.

An owl flapped past the moon. Lionel Kemp laughed as he thought of Julie Golden waking beside the murdered youth.

Julie squeezed her Greek lover's hand as fifty men assembled in the valley five miles out of town. Lit only by thin moonlight, she couldn't see their faces. But she had to trust them. It was the only way.

"Talk to them, Phillipas," she urged him.

The immigrant grunted and kissed her cheek.

As he addressed her army, Julie smiled and stood behind him, head bowed, as if she didn't understand what he was talking about. But the man's enflamed words, his call for the citizens of Oreville to take what was rightfully theirs and to bring renewed life to the town, even stirred her.

Julie studied his sharp gestures and self-assured posture. He was perfect, she thought. The kind of man others would follow. Phillipas had been born to it.

He promised them $100 each—more if they recovered a huge store of silver. The men cheered and thrust their rifles into the inky desert sky.

Julie closed her eyes. As soon as all this was over, she and Phillipas would ride into the desert with the silver, slowly making their way to California. It would be dangerous, of course. When Lionel realized that she'd betrayed him he'd stop at nothing to find her.

But Julie blocked out the dark thoughts and dreamed of a happy life as Phillipas Telonia whipped the crowd into a frenzy with his accented words.

Lionel Kemp, she thought, you've finally met your match.

Spur answered the knock on his door. He'd gotten out of bed at sunrise, shaved and dressed in clean clothing, so he greeted Mayor Kincaid with a hearty smile.

"McCoy, you may be right."

"Good morning to you, too. About what?"

"About the mine being attacked." Kincaid looked around the room. "I've heard rumors that several men left town last night. Dozens of them, all riding west. They could have been going to a meeting."

"I see." Spur frowned. "Possibly. Things like this have happened before. Angry men band together to take care of business. But I don't remember hearing about an all-out assault on any mine, especially a silver mine."

"Me neither, but I thought you should know. Keep me informed, McCoy."

"Thanks."

Spur thought hard as he closed the door. It didn't sound good. It didn't sound good at all. He considered questioning the men in town, but that wouldn't do much. Even if one of them admitted that there had been a meeting, and that the group was planning to take the mine, it wouldn't stop the battle.

McCoy had to warn Magnus. He had to be there just in case.

That morning, Julie heard her kitchen door bang open. She stifled a cry of surprise as Lionel Kemp stormed into the parlor. The beautiful woman rose from the settee, glanced down at Phillipas and ran to the dusty man.

"You're back early!" she said, smiling at him.

"No shit." Kemp growled and threw off his coat and hat. "Who the hell's he?"

"Ah, Lionel Kemp, meet Phillipas Telonia."

The immigrant rose and stretched out a hand, but Kemp turned to Julie.

"I'm her—"

"General!" she said, breaking off his words. "We organized everything last night—well, Phil did. I've got the men and he got them fired up. We're ready, Lionel!"

Kemp studied her face. "Really?"

"Yes." She forced a laugh. "Lionel, I knew I couldn't do it alone. Since I thought you'd be gone—after I received your telegram—I figured I had to have some help. That's when I met Phillipas." She smiled. "Pete introduced us. He's the best man for the job."

But as Kemp switched his gaze from the woman to the man, Julie felt herself dying inside. Lionel had come back. She'd have to stay home while they rode out to attack the mine. She wouldn't be able to leave with Phillipas. All her plans had crumbled to dust the moment Lionel had walked through her door. She'd never be rid of him.

"I'll make coffee." Julie walked into the sun-brightened kitchen. She made no move toward the coffee pot and didn't go outside to the well.

Make the best of it, she thought. Anything could happen before tomorrow night. Lionel might decide to leave after he had the silver. He might ride out before everything happened. Or she could have Phillipas kill him.

Kill him!

The thought unnerved her. Julie glanced around the spotless room. She remembered that night when she woke up with a headache beside the dead man. She'd always felt that Lionel had done it—one of his cruel tricks on her. But he'd almost been successful in convincing her otherwise.

He deserved to die for what he'd made her do.

Julie grabbed the coffee pot and slammed through the door. She furiously worked the pump handle, filled the metal container and returned to the kitchen.

After stoking the flames in the firebox she set the water on it to heat. Julie Golden sighed and walked into the parlor.

"Good. You've planned well, Telonia," Lionel was saying. "Almost as well as I would have done it."

"Thank you, Kemp." The Greek basked in the man's praise.

"But we'll have to cut the men's pay. I can't afford to give them each a hundred dollars—that'd be five thousand!" Lionel shook his head. "We'll cut it to fifty and not tell them until it's over."

Phillipas shifted on the settee. "That would be dangerous, Kemp. The men may turn against me—against you!"

Lionel laughed. "Leave it to me. I'll handle it."

Kemp rose from the settee, grabbed the bottle of whiskey from the table near the window and drank.

Julie nervously looked at Phillipas. Could she ask him to kill Lionel? And if so, would he do it? Of course he would, she told herself. She didn't know much about him, but he seemed so angry and lonely. Desperate. Haunted.

She fingered the curtains. Phillipas turned to her. His face was flushed with excitement. The Greek immigrant winked.

He'd do it if she told him that Lionel was lying to him, Julie thought. He'd kill the man if she told him that he was going to keep all the silver for himself.

When to ask him. Tonight? She couldn't risk it. If

Phillipas failed her she'd be in Lionel's power again, and that was something she couldn't face.

Not tonight!

CHAPTER TWELVE

"It's me, Mayor Kincaid!" Justin shouted as a rifle exploded not far from the riders. "Me and McCoy have to see Magnus! Let us pass!"

"Alright," the unseen guard said.

Spur grunted as they rode toward the mine. "You've got a hot state here, Kincaid," he said as heat shimmered from the sand below them.

The mayor took off his hat and slicked the sweat from his forehead with the back of his hand. "Hell. This is nothing. You're missing the really sizzling weather. Come back in two months, McCoy."

"No, thanks." He fixed his eyes on a dark slash on the mountain that marked the mine.

"You figure he'll believe us?" Kincaid asked.

"I don't know. He's so worried about guarding his silver that he'll probably act as if the threat is real. That's the kind of man he seems to be."

Kincaid guffawed. "Come on, McCoy. You only

met him once. How'd you know that?"

Spur squinted into the sun. "I know men like him. Lots of them. But I wish I knew who Lionel was— the man who sent that telegram to Julie Golden that started this whole thing."

"Back to Lionel again? Hmm. I was figuring it was a first name. But maybe not." Justin Kincaid bit his lip. "Then again there's Lionel Kemp."

McCoy looked at him. "Who's that?"

"Used to be the biggest landowner in Oreville. Owned the fanciest saloons. After the mines started closing he lost a shitload of money. Abandoned a lot of his property, withdrew every dime he had from the banks and sold most of his businesses." Mayor Kincaid met Spur's gaze. His left eye twitched.

"What is it?"

"Lionel Kemp sold the Motherlode Saloon. To Julie Golden."

Spur took in the words. "What happened to him?"

"Hell, I don't know. He sorta dropped out of sight. Haven't seen him around town. Rumor says that he's pretty close to Julie, but he moved out of his house."

Their mounts picked their way carefully over the rocky ground. Spur wished he had a cheroot. "A man who's lost that much money might be pushed to desperate acts."

"Agreed," Kincaid said. "Maybe you're right, McCoy. Maybe Lionel's been using Julie as some kind of organizer to handle the silver robberies. I doubt if she's actually done any of them, but she could be involved in other ways."

"Doing Kemp's dirty work for him." Spur shook his head. "Willingly?"

"Who knows? Let's just get out to the mine. If you're right about the telegram, Magnus might lose more than one shipment of silver tonight!"

They kicked their horses' flanks, urging the protesting beasts into a trot as soon as the ground smoothed into sand broken by scrub and short dunes. As they rode, Spur tried to picture the beautiful woman sending out men with orders to steal and to kill. If she was responsible, this Kemp must have been forcing her to do it. But how?

"Come on, Isabella," Kincaid said. "You got a new shoe, and we'll water you as soon as we get to the mine. Don't let me down, girl!"

Spur grinned at the mayor." Shit, Justin; you talk to that thing as if she was human."

Kincaid looked at him with a curious smile.

A half hour later they'd rubbed down their horses and followed their escort to Cleve Magnus.

"What brings you two out here?" he asked.

"Trouble, Magnus." Spur paced. "I don't know how to tell you this, but there's every possibility that an army will assault your mine."

"What?" The big jowled man pulled on a glass of whiskey, coughed and sighed.

"Tonight. This guy who's been taking your silver isn't satisfied with a shipment or two. He wants to clean you out and he's hired himself a lot of men to do it."

The mine owner poured himself another drink, carefully placed the top on the decanter and pushed it away. He downed the liquor in one gulp. "Okay."

Kincaid glanced at Spur and then looked at

Magnus. "Okay? Just okay? Cleve, didn't you hear what the man said?"

"Sure I heard him!" Magnus snorted. "I've been thinking something like this would happen. The men in Oreville are so broke they're losing their minds." He stared hard at McCoy. "How sure are you of this?"

"As sure as I can be. Information's sketchy. I've put it together from what I have."

Magnus nodded. "I can't ignore the threat. Okay, I'll take steps. No one would be so stupid to attack during the day, so it'll have to be at night. I'll cancel the evening shifts and alert everyone, station extra guards around this building. Since this is where I store the smelted silver, they'll head here first. I'll have every man armed and on the alert by dusk."

"Might be a good idea to stock up on extra ammunition," Spur said. "You'll need it."

"Good idea. I'll have a few men ride into town."

"Tell them to act casually, not to attract any attention. If we can make the thieves think they're surprising us, it'll be to our advantage."

"Right!" Magnus stood and rubbed his palms together.

"Hell, Cleve. Are you looking forward to this? An all-out war?"

"In a way. By tomorrow it'll all be over. I won't have to worry about any of this. Either way, win or lose, it's history."

"We're not sure anything's going to happen," Spur added, "but you're doing the right thing."

Magnus pounded on his desk. "Frankie!" he bellowed. .

A fresh-faced youth instantly appeared in the doorway. "Yes, boss?"

"Come with me. We've got work to do!" He turned to his visitors. "You boys sticking around?"

"Thought we might, if you don't mind. I've got some ideas on how to defend this place."

"Defend the mine?" Frankie rolled his eyes. "Shit, boss; what's happening?"

"Either the end of the world, or the light at the end of the tunnel. Come on!"

"It's time."

Julie started at Lionel's words. She watched, helplessly, as he and Phillipas checked their gear— ammo bags, rifles, revolvers.

"Is there anything I can do?" Julie asked.

"Yes." Phillipas turned to her, "Pray for us."

She bit her thumb. "You two be careful out there, you hear me?"

Kemp laughed. "Don't worry your pretty little head about me. We'll be back before you know it."

They walked out the door and mounted up. She watched from the window until they were lost in the evening's darkness.

Julie slumped onto the settee. She nearly dissolved into tears. Lionel hadn't left her for a second since he'd arrived. He and Phillipas spent the whole day planning the attack. They even went together to relieve themselves. She hadn't had a single chance to talk privately with Phillipas.

So he wouldn't kill Lionel. They'd attack the mine, get the silver, and come back. Kemp would send Phillipas away and she'd live in bondage for the rest of her life.

Julie wrung her hands. This wasn't what she'd planned.

The door burst open. The woman caught her breath as Phillipas stepped in. Julie ran to him and groaned as he wrapped his arms around her.

"I forgot my kerchief," he said, kissing her neck.

"Phillipas, I—"

"I have to leave, Julie."

"I know. I know! But Phillipas!"

He held her at arm's length. "What?"

Looking into his eyes, she shook her head. "You be careful out there."

"I will. Goodbye."

He was gone again.

She hadn't been able to do it. Her resolve had disappeared as soon as she saw his expression. As much as Julie Golden hated Lionel Kemp, she wasn't a savage. She couldn't order the man's murder.

The woman sat by the window, determined to stay there until she saw the two men in her life riding back with their prize.

Dusk. Spur was satisfied with Magnus' preparations. He'd been careful not to make any obvious changes. To the untrained eye, it looked as if it was business as usual at the mine. A few men were stationed at each end of the rusty iron track that led from the mouth of the shaft's entrance to the smelting plant. They pushed a car back and forth, up and down. It was impossible to see that it was empty from a distance.

No more kerosene lamps than usual flickered from the trees and buildings scattered around the place. Smoke rose from the bunkhouse, the cookhouse and the other major structures, while it belched from the spiraled chimneys rising from the building that housed the smelting operation.

Looking over the desert, Cleve Magnus, Justin Kincaid and Spur McCoy had one last discussion before their final meeting with the men.

"The attack could come at any time," Spur said. "We may be warned by shots from the desert, either from the perimeter guards or into them. Or they may bypass the guards. Either way, they have to approach from the desert. The hills are too steep to mount a successful attack from the rear."

He turned to look at the shoulder of the mountain on which the mine—and they were situated.

"We've agreed that it would be best to have one-third of the men to the southwest, stationed behind bushes and rocks. To the right, the northeastern side, another eighteen men will wait. The rest'll stay in the camp itself to guard it, out of sight but at the ready. Is everything clear?" Spur asked.

The men grunted affirmatively.

"Great. Magnus, go talk to your men. Have them in position in five minutes!"

"Will do."

As the short man trotted off, Kincaid turned to Spur. "You know, we may be doing all this for nothing."

"I know." He grabbed a cheroot from the mayor's coat pocket and lit it with a lucifer. "But this is my job."

Cleve Magnus had 53 men at the mine. Kemp was counting on having surprise on his side. Spur hoped that foreknowledge would be in their favor.

If anything happened . . . .

They waited.

Magnus huffed back to them. The three men crouched behind the line of water barrels that rimmed the porch of the main house. Eight armed men were at the ready inside. Every other man was at his station, but an eyeball check told Spur that they had been well hidden.

"Good work, Magnus."

The man grunted. "What'd you expect? This ain't poker, for Chrissakes!"

Three hours later they were still waiting. Their talk had ceased. McCoy felt the men's edginess, the tension that rippled the air behind the barrels where they squatted.

Spur kicked out a cramp that had flared in his leg, maintaining his continuous scan of the desert floor below them.

A rifle boomed in the distance. The explosion split open the night silence. McCoy peered into the darkness as the sound echoed off the sheer cliffs behind them.

"The first guard?" Kincaid asked beside him.

"Maybe."

"Do you think—?" Magnus began.

Spur shook his head. He checked his Winchester for the thousandth time as Cleve and Justin squirmed beside him.

Another rifle blast shook the area. Closer this time. Much closer.

Straining his ears, Spur heard unmistakable

sounds of a mass of horses approaching the mine.
He couldn't see them but they sure were out there.

He'd been right. Somehow, he'd been right!

Spur grinned at the wary Kincaid and Justin.
"You boys ready for a fight?"

"Yeah. Let me at the bastards!" Cleve said.

"Then let's give them an old fashioned welcome."

Spur twisted to his side. One of Magnus's men
ducked out of sight behind a pile of wooden crates.

Everything was ready.

The first shots had been fired.

CHAPTER THIRTEEN

A thin, high cloud passed before the first quarter moon. Spur hunkered down behind the rain barrels and fruitlessly surveyed the desert floor that lay beyond the mining operation. As his eyes adjusted to the darkness he began to make out shapes against the light ground—clumps of rocks, stunted juniper trees. Two minutes after he'd heard the rifle blasts nothing had happened.

McCoy turned to Cleve Magnus. "You told your men not to show themselves too early, right? They'll hold off shooting until they're right here?"

"Yes, damnit!" the miner said. "Hell, isn't this thing ever going to start?"

"It already has. Listen, Magnus! The horses are getting closer."

Two-hundred hooves pounded the sand. Spur finally saw the moving bulk that approached the hillside mine. They were much less than a mile away.

"That's them," Mayor Kincaid said. "Damn if you weren't right, McCoy!"

He softly grunted. "Like I told you, that's my job. Get set, men."

By the sparkling light of the moon, Spur watched as the mass of riders parted in the middle. "They're breaking up into two groups," he said, wondering what Kemp had promised them for the night's work.

"I know, I know; I got eyes!" Magnus said. "Jeeeezus!"

"Shut up!" Kincaid's voice was low.

It began all at once. A front of ten riders stormed up the hill and launched an all-out attack on the mine. A second wave of ten more men charged onto Magnus's operation. After the first of their rounds had slammed into the house, Magnus's men fired on them from around the camp, blasting deadly messengers into the oncomers.

Spur slammed a slug into a townsman as he rode toward the house. He blasted away with a cursing Kincaid and a jubilant Magnus. The air filled with the sharp scent of gunpowder. Blinding explosions easily revealed the positions of Magnus's men.

But Spur wasn't surprised that the army began to scatter. The undertrained men obviously hadn't been prepared for this. Lack of discipline killed their united strength, breaking it into pockets of offense.

Pain-wracked men died as they slid from their horses. Spur spent two minutes firing and reloading his Winchester, bobbing above the triple-thick line of barrels that Magnus had had filled with sand, ducking back to safety; endlessly repeating the routine.

"Shit! They mean business!" Kincaid said.

"So do we!" McCoy said. "Come on, mayor! Where's your backbone?"

"Trying real hard to stay in one place!"

The front line of barrels splintered before them. Spur picked off as many of the attackers as he could, but the dim light and the horses' frenzied reaction to the battle blazing around them made accuracy difficult at best.

The second group of townsmen had split again. Some distance away, Spur heard the two other groups clashing with the men Magnus had planted on either side of the mine to stave off any entrance from those sides.

"Yeah!" McCoy said as five riderless horses ran from the area, trampling the dead men that lay littered on the ground. Of the twenty men who'd stormed them, Spur counted seven still on horseback and one dashing madly back into the desert. He let him go; he was harmless.

As McCoy expertly broke open his Winchester and reloaded, an attacker pumped out two shots as he streaked past them. Cleve Magnus howled and dropped his weapon.

"Damn shit!"

Spur grimaced. Leaving the safety of the barrier, he dashed along the right side of the house and pounded up toward the rear. He'd aimed even before the rider who'd plugged Magnus flashed by.

The deadly bullet slammed into the man's chest as he rode past, instantly killing him.

Spur trotted back to the others. The fighting was less violent. "Where'd you get hit, Magnus?"

"Hell, McCoy. It's only my arm." The miner grabbed his rifle. "I'm gonna get those bastards!"

"You can still handle that thing?" Spur asked as he fired at a mounted attacker. He missed.

"Sure as I'm Cleve P. Magnus!"

The level of gunfire quickly fell off. The three remaining attackers surveyed the scene and rode hell-bent away from the mine. Spur blasted a parting shot at them for good measure.

"What's the 'P' stand for?" Justin asked.

Shouts and victorious cheers from the men stationed around the camp drowned out the mine owner's answer. Fighting on the two flanks eased off as well.

"What did you say, Cleve?" the mayor asked.

"Holy shit! No time for talk, boys!"

A wave of eight fresh riders, probably funneled from the secondary positions, exploded around them. Spur, Kincaid and a barely functional Magnus managed to pick off two of them, while their compatriots routed five more. But the agonized screams issuing from various parts of the camp meant that Magnus was losing men, too.

The riders soon tired of their exposed positions. They dismounted and scattered to prepare for an all-out fight. At least one of them was surprised by one of Magnus's men who killed him as he dropped from his saddle behind a pile of broken ore.

"Persistent little devils, aren't they?" Kincaid said.

"Yeah."

Spur blasted a waist-high boulder behind one of the attackers. The lead ricocheted and slammed into a townsman as he ducked behind an overturned wagon.

"Lucky shot," Magnus said, groaning from his wound.

"Luck? Hell, I planned that!"

Three separate battles turned the sky into a series of brilliant explosions. Smoke hung thickly throughout the camp. Kincaid blasted two of the three men to hell as Spur finished off the other one.

In the distance, he noted several riders rapidly departing, heading for Oreville in defeat.

"That's it for them," McCoy said.

Magnus let out a piercing whistle.

"What's that for?" Spur asked.

"You'll see."

Two of the man's workers—"Crack shots," Magnus proudly said—emerged from their hiding places and approached the bodies. They quickly removed weapons and checked for signs of life.

Their battle was over. Spur rose to his feet with Kincaid and Magnus. He turned to gaze at the war still raging to the southeast. Two men on horseback charged up to the main area of the camp.

"Shit! Haven't they had enough? Those boys just won't quit!" Magnus said, rubbing his arm.

Seeing the men standing around the building, they turned north toward the face of the mountain. Spur cursed as they dashed behind the cookhouse out of the line of fire.

"They can't go far," he said, and bolted.

Spur pounded the dirt with his boots. He'd just

reloaded so he had two easy shots before he had to get busy again. As he passed the cookhouse Spur picked off one of the fleeing men. He plummeted to the ground and rolled to a stop.

The other rider kicked his mount's flanks, urging him on. Huffing, Spur raced up the mountain beside the iron tracks. He ducked as the attacker took a wild shot behind him. The riderless horse sped past.

He could have only one destination. In. Into the mine.

Spur lateralled across the rough road as the attacker flew into the wooden supported mine entrance. Too far away for a good shot, he lowered his aim.

It was only a matter of time, he thought. Just one entrance to the mine—Magnus had briefed him on that. He had to wait.

The camp was quiet below him. Spur filled the empty chamber and tapped his boot heel. The fighting had ended. Standing out of direct fire, he wasn't surprised to hear the kerosene lamps inside blast into darkness with the gunman's ammunition.

Spur was suddenly weary. "Come on out, asshole! I hold all the cards. It's time we all went home."

Silence.

McCoy dislodged a gnarled juniper bush from the bone dry dirt. Hefting it in his hand, he threw it before the narrow mine opening.

Two explosions echoed from inside. Light flashed along the steel car railings as the tree fell to the ground.

"Damn!"

Spur smiled at the man's voice. "Out of ammunition? Get your ass out here, man! I won't kill you in cold blood. You'll get a fair trial."

Again, nothing. He was betting that the attacker had used up his ammo but couldn't depend on that. And McCoy had the feeling that he wouldn't be able to talk the man out.

What to do?

Spur produced a lucifer from his coat pocket. He picked up a small rock and held the tip of the match at its rough surface. He waited.

The horse moved inside the mine. The sound of its hooves grew louder. A second before it emerged from the mine, Spur struck the match and threw it onto the dead juniper. The oil-rich bush burst into an inferno. Suddenly faced with the whirling tower of fire, the advancing horse reared back in terror, sending its rider hurling to the dust.

Spur grabbed the man before he could get up. He locked his hands around the attacker's arms behind his back.

"Walk!" he bellowed.

"Damn you!"

He was thin but strong. With an effort, Spur pushed him down the mountain as the old juniper crackled and roared behind them. It was too easy, Spur thought as he forced the man into the camp. He hadn't even tried to get free. Of course, he was probably just a simple townsman who'd been trying to earn a few dollars. The guy was probably scared stiff.

"You got one of them?" Kincaid asked as he ran up, rifle dangling from his right hand.

"Yep."

"Who is that?" The mayor grabbed the gunman's chin and jerked it up. "Shit!" he said, moving closer. "I'll be. It's Lionel Kemp!"

Spur automatically tightened his grip. "The ringleader, eh? You didn't plan this party very well, Kemp. But we tried to make you feel welcome. Come on!"

McCoy ran the man into the camp, the mayor taking up the rear.

Cleve P. Magnus met them. "Jesus, McCoy! Twenty of my good, loyal men are dead!"

"You've got Kemp here to thank for that. Get me some rope!" he barked.

One of Magnus's hired hands threw him a coil. Spur slipped one end under Lionel's wrists and quickly knotted a firm knot. The man sullenly refused to talk as he was trussed up.

"That should hold him," Spur said.

"Yeah. Now we gotta find a good tree for the lynching." Cleve surveyed the bare ground around the buildings. "Shit! No trees out here in the desert!"

Spur grunted. "There's not going to be any lynching."

"No? Then I'm gonna blast his guts out!" Cleve Magnus swung up his rifle.

"Drop your weapon, Magnus! Hasn't there been enough killing?"

"Not quite!" He laughed.

Kincaid grabbed the wounded man's good shoulder. "You're not thinking straight. Hell, you've got a hole in your left arm for Godsakes! Cleve, you do this and you'll hang for murder."

"Who's gonna convict me? You? Let me go!"

Lionel looked up at the man and spat in his face. Magnus blubbered, his short body shaking with unmitigated rage.

"Damn you all!" he said.

"Take this," McCoy said, thrusting the loose end of the rope that bound Kemp's hands toward the mayor. Spur kicked the Spencer from Magnus's hands and landed a clean punch to the mine owner's chin. Cleve spun and slowly sank to the ground.

"Just what he needed," Spur said.

"You can't blame him, McCoy. I'd probably do the same thing." He drew the rope taut. "I don't like this animal you've given me. Here, you take him!"

Spur caught the rope. Lionel stared at the ground.

"Gotta get him back to town. You going with me?" Spur asked.

"Ah, well, I guess so. But there's a lot to be done here." He looked around the camp.

"Someone should send for the barber. He'll be happy as a pig in shit to have some work to do." Spur looked at the row of eight sitting, wounded men, and the bodies that lay sprawled around the camp.

"Yeah. Okay. Just a minute." The mayor grabbed a bucket and poured it onto Magnus's face.

He exploded into consciousness, blowing the liquid from his lips, shaking his head and shoulders. The mine owner slowly rose to his feet. "Jesus," he said, rubbing his chin. "What happened to me?"

"You ran into a fist," Spur said.

"And a bullet," Kincaid added.

"You lost your head, Magnus. Me and the mayor

are taking Kemp back into town. Give us any more trouble and you'll pay for it."

"Uh, yeah. God, I need a drink!" The mine owner turned toward his wounded men.

After placing the bound man on a horse, Spur and Kincaid mounted up and led him from the camp.

The first few miles were slow, but aquamarine eventually tinted the eastern sky. They quickened their horses' pace as dawn broke over the desert.

"What's Julie Golden to you?" Spur asked the sullen Lionel Kemp. When no answer issued from the man, Spur asked again.

Kemp sighed and shrugged. "She's a girl, a pretty girl who robbed that bastard's silver for me for quite a while. I underestimated her," he said.

"Yeah. But she was working for you. She didn't do anything directly?"

Lionel glanced at McCoy. "She sucked my dick—that was about all."

Spur quieted Kincaid's instant guffaw with a sharp look. "This war was your plan, then."

"Yeah. It was all mine." He jerked his head. "How the hell did you know about it?"

"I've got my ways, Kemp. When a rat's planning to raid the pantry, you can smell the stink. No, it wasn't one of your men. I don't know how you conned them into doing your dirty work, but I'm happy to report as many as ten of them wised up and rode back into town."

"Yeah. They were a big help."

"Say, McCoy; we might meet up with some of them on the way." The mayor tapped the butt of the rifle he'd slung over his shoulder.

"It's possible. But I don't think it'll be us they're shooting at."

Lionel grunted.

They rode on.

A half hour later they were following a trail of blood. The liquid had created reddish-brown stains on the sand. As they increased their distance from the camp the droplets enlarged. Soon McCoy and Kincaid saw the dead body.

"You happy, Kemp?"

"Shut up!"

"It's one thing to steal some silver here and there. It's another thing to have an eighth of the town's men killed for your petty appetite for money."

"I don't have to listen to this!" he shouted, wrestling on his mount.

"Like hell you don't," Spur said. "We're gonna fill your ears until we get back to Oreville. It could be worse; we could have let Magnus fill you with lead."

"That might have been better."

Spur smiled. "Kincaid!"

The mayor glanced at him through the increasing daylight. "I was just wondering what that damn 'P' stands for in Magnus's name. But what is it?" The mayor shook his head.

"You know a shorter way back to town than this Godforsaken chicken scratch?" Spur asked.

The mayor scratched his chin. "Yep. The old Indian trail. Isn't used much, kinda dangerous in places."

"Let's take it. The sooner we get this man locked up, the better!"

"Okay."

Spur followed the mayor's lead, turning west. "We'll dump him in the post office. That means we really have to find some place to move Melissa and Emma, but that shouldn't be too much of a problem anymore."

"Yeah. What about Julie Golden?"

McCoy hesitated. The bound man riding in front of him slightly turned his head at the woman's name. "I don't know. I'll have to question her. Kemp here's admitted to doing everything."

"She hired her own men to steal Magnus's silver," Lionel said. "I just put her up to it. I never pulled one single robbery."

"But you received the goods," Spur suggested. He snorted.

"I don't know, Kincaid," McCoy said to the mayor. "I'll figure it out when I have to."

"Fair enough."

Fifteen minutes later, their mounts entered rocky terrain. The once smooth desert floor broke up into jutting hills, yawning cracks and huge piles of boulders. It was rougher riding but Spur was satisfied that he'd taken the correct course. He wanted Kemp off his hands as soon as possible.

"I warned you," the mayor said as they passed a difficult stretch of land. "This ain't the way to a church picnic. Which reminds me about the ladies' social I missed."

At that instant, Lionel Kemp stabbed his mount's flanks with his heels. The beast launched into a run, racing for the edge of a hill ten yards away.

"Damn!"

Spur unslung his rifle. Before he could get a bead on him, the man had dropped out of sight. Angry at himself, McCoy urged his horse to a run.

"No. Wait! The Merrone!" Kincaid yelled.

Ignoring the man's cry, he quickly cleared the land.

Spur couldn't halt his horse in time. He flew from the animal's back as he fell ten feet and plunged into a white water river. The world tumbled and bubbled around him. He couldn't breathe.

CHAPTER FOURTEEN

Spur spun in the surprisingly strong current of the Merrone River. It's icy water drilled into his skin like a Chinatown doctor's needles, prickling him all over. Holding his breath, he clawed for the bank and searched for a foothold, not knowing which way was up as the water tossed his body in all directions.

McCoy saw his frightened horse's legs paddle by. Furious at this unexpected turn of events, he righted himself and broke through the surface of the churning water.

Air blasted from his mouth and nose. He panted, wiped the Nevada liquid from his eyes and blinked at the sight of the retreating figure riding the water away from him. Lionel Kemp shot down the Merrone.

Spur cursed and reached for his rifle. It was gone, of course. The impact of his body falling into the river had knocked it from where he had slung it over his shoulder. It could be halfway to Oreville by now.

Weaponless, McCoy lunged into the current. He struggled to force his chilled limbs to move. Dusting off his ancient swimming skills, slicing with his hands, Spur rode with the river, keeping just his eyes above the water to watch Lionel's escape.

The man was clever, Spur admitted to himself. He heard Kemp's laughter over the rush of the water. The bursts of wild, crazed guffaws infuriated him.

The riverbed slammed against his feet. He stumbled on the slippery rocks, splashed and tore his way toward the criminal, half-swimming, half-walking.

The rock walls that the river had cut into the desert floor drew closer together on both sides. Spur struggled through the speeding water. Kemp's head dipped out of sight several times. Faster, McCoy told himself. Faster!

A quick look at the edge of the cliff to his left showed nothing but the barren ridge of earth. Mayor Kincaid must be following him up there somewhere, but Spur couldn't rely on him. Besides, he wouldn't need any help if he could just get his hands around Kemp's scrawny little neck.

Spur held his breath as a wall of water slapped into his face. He blew it out and dragged himself through the Merrone. His clothes had turned to lead. Even though the Secret Service agent was moving with the current, the extra weight hindered his progress. Spur shrugged off the sodden jacket and ripped his shirt from his torso.

Lionel Kemp rose and dropped from sight sixty feet in front of him. Worn rocks pierced the boiling water's surface ahead. Beyond that, he couldn't see the river. A small fall, Spur wondered? He'd find out soon enough.

The Merrone pulled him along with incredible strength. McCoy held his breath and slid head-first over a smooth boulder. He felt his body shoot into the air and violently plummet into a deep pool.

The dive sent him to the bottom. Spur slammed his hands against the slimy rocks to prevent a broken nose, jacknifed and pushed off them. He surfaced and blew out his breath.

Rattled but unharmed, he wiped his eyes. Fifteen feet away he saw the wet bootprints that marked Lionel's escape from the river. They led onto a sandbar that jutted into a bend in the water flowing from the pool and disappeared into a thicket of cottonwoods.

Great!

Spur swam to the bank, walked up its gently sloped surface and strode into the trees. He slapped water from his pants, shivering.

"Give it up, Kemp!" he yelled.

"Not on your life!"

Spur heard the man's thrashings through the underbrush and saplings that sucked water from the earth bordering the river. McCoy brushed back short trees on either side, set his jaw and huffed as the light from the rising sun slowly filtered through the leaves, warming his body.

He worked through his exhaustion, finding additional stores of energy. After all, this wasn't the first time he'd gone without sleep.

The accumulation of hundreds of years of dead leaves and fallen branches slowed his steps. Every three feet he repeated the painstaking process of pushing one boot into the unstable mulch and retreating his other foot from the hole he'd plowed into it behind him.

It was slowing Kemp's movements too, Spur thought as a stiff twig scraped his bare chest. He barely noticed the pain of dry wood entering his toughened skin.

"You're making me mad, Kemp!" he bellowed.

Lionel returned nothing but the crashes of his frantic escape.

Spur grimaced and continued his slow progress. The trees grew more thickly. Their trunks crowded each other and inumerable saplings strained to grow in the thin light. Spur saw hints of bare sand through their trunks on either side. The cottonwoods must be following an underground stream, he thought. Kemp would use the trees for cover as long as he could. Unarmed, without a horse, the man would never be so stupid as to run into the featureless desert.

No. He was going to make this as hard as possible.

A sharpened spear of wood shot through the air from the forest ahead. With no time to react, Spur gasped as it grazed his left shoulder.

"Damn!" he yelled. The man must have been whittling as he moved.

Two more deadly spears plowed into trees inches from his naked torso. Furious, Spur dug them out and hurled the pointed sticks back into the forest ahead. "I've had it with you, Lionel Kemp!"

Spur redoubled his efforts, crashing faster and faster through the undergrowth and leathery leaves. No more spears showed themselves. He instinctively stopped after five more yards.

The forest was silent save for the sound of an early morning breeze which stirred the cottonwoods' leaves into gentle motion. Kemp wasn't moving.

Where was he?

Spur searched the woods. The ground seemed clearer, as if a devil wind had swept through the trees from the desert floor, scouring it of some of the dead leaves. A spangled trail of water still stretched before him, clearly marking Kemp's joyous passage, but it was thinner, less visible. They were both drying off.

Had the man set a trap?

McCoy weighed his options. He would walk into whatever Kemp had waiting for him, hoping his wits would save his hide. He could break out into the desert, circle ahead and try to surprise him.

Or he could stand there and wait.

Rage shot through his veins. Spur trudged forward, pivoting his head with every step, searching the trees with his trained eyes. Color flashed through the trees ten feet ahead. Lionel had been wearing a red checkered shirt. Must be him.

McCoy warily approached, moving as slowly and quietly as he could through the aggravating leaves. Though there were fewer of them they crunched with every step.

He glanced at a dead tree trunk that lay across the ground. The fallen tree had created a wedge in the mulch. It might be a good foothold. It led somewhat toward that place where he'd seen the shirt, which had now vanished.

Fixing his eyes onto the spot so that he didn't lose it in the tangled confusion of luxuriant growth, Spur stepped onto the log. It didn't shift, so he inched along it. A color alien to the natural vegetation showed itself again.

Closer. Spur broadened his pace. Perfectly balanced on the four-inch thick trunk, he slipped to its end and pushed through the trees.

McCoy almost laughed as he saw Kemp's shirt hanging above his head. The bastard had slipped the buckle end of his belt around an overhead branch and attached his shirt to the other end. The wind had created the illusion of movement.

It took Spur one second to sum up the situation. Instantly alert, he searched the surrounding trees and saw nothing.

Kemp wasn't there. He'd set up the diversion and it had worked. Cursing the day he'd ever heard of Oreville, Spur blindly stumbled through the trees. The fallen leaves were so jumbled that they showed no trail. Kemp could be anywhere.

But he hadn't heard the man move. True, Lionel enjoyed a short lead. But still . . . .

Spur stopped. A rustling ten feet from him quickly halted. Kemp was walking with him to cover the sound of his escape. He was crafty, McCoy thought. But not crafty enough.

Spur pinpointed the location of the sound and raced toward it. He moved faster, surer. He finally had his first clear view of Lionel Kemp as the man ran like hell.

Increasing amounts of light filtered through the

trees. As they neared the open desert, Spur gained on the man but couldn't get within arm's reach.

The two men burst into the desert. McCoy gave it full steam. He easily overtook the man, slammed his hands around Kemp's torso and flung him onto the dirt like a sack of flour.

Lionel scrambled to his feet with a groan and assumed a boxer's stance.

"Come on. Put 'em up!" he jeered.

Unprepared for the boot that Spur drove into his jaw, Kemp reeled back and fell.

McCoy jumped onto his chest, grabbed Lionel's head with his left hand and pounded the man's face until his knuckles drew blood. The feeling of his fist smashing into Kemp's kisser was so satisfying after all the trouble the man had caused him.

Lionel's lips split. He struggled against Spur's blows as his eyes puffed and his chin cracked beneath one of McCoy's better placed punches. Kemp quieted and lay still beneath him. McCoy finally released the bloodied man's head. It dropped onto the sand.

Spur wearily rose from the unconscious man's chest and stood. A howl of pure pleasure ripped from his throat. After his quick celebration he knelt and grabbed Kemp's wrist. The man was still alive. His pulse was regular. He'd simply gone into shock and passed out.

Satisfied that he hadn't killed him, McCoy stuck his fist on his hips and looked at the desert. He didn't have a clue where he was, how far he'd ridden the Merrone or the location of the trail back to Oreville.

A turkey vulture, alerted by the smell of fresh

blood, wound through the sky overhead in a lazy downward spiral.

Now what?

"McCoy!"

The word crept on him from a distance. He saw a rider approaching. It called his name again and waved a kerchief wagging hand.

Spur smiled. Kincaid.

The faint sight of a second rider behind the mayor surprised and pleased him. They'd need more than one horse to get the three of them out of there.

McCoy squatted beside Kemp. He watched scarlet drops of blood slide from the man's face, fall onto the sand and sizzle in the sun.

Justin Kincaid rode up a minute later. "I'll be damned," the mayor said. "I thought I'd lost you!"

"Never underestimate the Secret Service," Spur smiled.

Kincaid stared down at Kemp's torn face from his mount. "Hoowhee! Must've been some furious fight. But you look pretty good. Not too busted up."

"Let's just say it was one-sided."

Kincaid humorously grunted.

"Who's that I saw riding behind you?" Spur asked.

"What?" The mayor twisted. "I don't know. I came here alone!"

The rider halted ten feet from them.

"Magnus!" Spur shouted as the dust settled onto the ground. "What in hell are you doing out here?"

The sweating miner pumped death into Kemp's chest with his rifle. The sound of the explosions rattled through the desert.

Kincaid stiffened. "Cleve, I warned you that—"

Spur grabbed the mayor's arm. "Forget it, Justin."

"But—but—"

"I killed him," he whispered. "He was already dead."

Kincaid nodded at McCoy as Magnus dismounted and trotted up to them.

"He's dead, ain't he?" the miner said, standing beside the body.

"Yeah. You won't be losing any more of your hard earned silver to that bastard."

Magnus sighed and kicked Lionel Kemp's lifeless body. "Look what you made me do!" he yelled. "Your money-hungry greed turned me into a savage! Made me kill you! Christ, it's just what I always promised myself I wouldn't do. Even though I lived out here with gunmen and lawlessness, I always tried to live a fairly clean life."

Spur cleared his throat. "Ah, Magnus, I don't think—"

"He's dead. It's over." The miner turned to the mayor. "Okay, Justin. Lock me up. Just like you said. I'm ready to face the consequences of my actions."

The mayor glanced at McCoy and slapped Magnus's back. "Forget it, Cleve," he said.

"What're you trying to do to me? McCoy, you got jurisdiction here. Order him to arrest me!"

"He won't do it. Look, Magnus. I'll let you go scot-free. But there's one condition," Justin said.

Spur stood back, crossed his arms and scratched the annoying wound in his chest.

"What's that?"

Kincaid grinned. "That you tell me what the

damn 'P' in your name stands for!''

"Well jeez, Justin!" Magnus threw off his hat, ground it into the dust and thought. "What the hell. I guess it was my right to shoot down the bastard, after what he did to me. After all those men he killed, all that silver he stole from me. Right?"

Spur nodded. "I suppose so."

"Then what the hell." He smiled and pushed his face toward the mayor's. "Okay, okay. Phineas."

The mayor jerked back. "What'd you call me?"

"No, no. Phineas. The 'P' stands for Phineas!"

Spur guffawed along with Kincaid. "Phineas?" he said. "Your parents must have hated you."

Magnus shook his head. "Come on. Let's get the hell out of here. I still need that drink!"

"Not so fast, Magnus. Who gets to take Kemp's body on his horse?" Spur asked.

The miner looked at it. "Can't we just leave him here? Hell, the buzzards'll be out in force in no time. By tomorrow morning he'll be picked clean."

Spur looked at the dead man. "No. The law's the law," he said, as sunlight glinted off the two red pools on Lionel Kemp's chest.

CHAPTER FIFTEEN

"Sorry, no haircuts today," Blair yelled as he heard the door to his barbershop bang open. "Come back next year!"

"I don't want a cut after the lousy job you did last time." Spur dropped the body that had been Lionel Kemp onto the crowded floor.

The sweating man turned and groaned. "Hell! Put that thing somewhere else! You hear me!" Blair kicked the lifeless form toward the door. "Can't you see I'm up to my ass in bodies, both living and dead?"

He was. His barber shop/surgery/undertaker's operation was overflowing with customers. Spur acknowledged a few of the wounded men that he recognized as Magnus's workers.

"Hell, it's not a rush job," McCoy said. "He won't be going anywhere."

"And neither will I. Chrissakes. How can I

possibly finish all this work? Cleaning, cutting, stitching—and that's just on the ones that's still breathing." The barber squatted beside a man, splashed whiskey into his chest wound and dug for the bullet. The patient's face turned white. "I don't even wanna think about all the bodies they're bringing by wagon from the silver mine. Shit! Why wasn't I a bartender? You know, a clean job?"

"No adventure."

The barbership smelled of the effects of violence —sweat, alcohol and blood.

"You get him fit for burial, you hear? As a government agent, I'm ordering you to do your duty."

"Then you better rustle up some help for me. I don't have the time to make any more plain coffins. Now git!"

Spur turned from the scene of carnage and walked into the sun.

Mayor Justin Kincaid hurried toward him. "I just checked, McCoy," he said, out of breath. "Seems one of the first of Kemp's men who returned to town last night spread the word on what was happening out at the mine. A citizens' committee was formed. They nabbed the rascals as they rode in with their tails between their legs. Got seven of 'em locked up in the post office."

Spur grunted.

"There's still one we haven't found. A Greek fella. He was a general or something."

"Hmm. What about Melissa and Emma Grieve? They're not in there with all those—"

Kincaid smiled. "Naw. They're back in their hotel room at the Eastern Heights, now that they're out of danger."

McCoy lifted his left eyebrow. "And Julie Golden? What about her?"

"Damn! Didn't think about Ma. I don't know where she is. Maybe you better—"

"Yeah." Spur walked to the Motherlode.

Julie found herself suffocating. She pushed against the heavy, sweating flesh that pinned her to the bed and gently skidded to one side on the cool sheet.

He was so handsome, she thought, listening to Phillipas Telonia's rhythmic snores. Julie threw off the covers and rested her head on his chest. His strong, regular heartbeat was soothing.

She'd waited beside the window last night for hours. After chastising herself for sitting and doing nothing, Julie had walked into the cool air and yanked weeds from her kitchen garden by moonlight.

Every five minutes or so, she'd turned toward the east and searched the sky for any signs of the war that raged there. Though she saw nothing, Julie had felt as if she were there in the middle of it.

In truth, she was. Why hadn't she left town? After Lionel had gone the first time she could have taken the stage, leaving everything behind but what she could carry with her. But then she'd met Phillipas and everything had changed.

Julie had screamed as her kitchen door banged open at midnight. Her general had thrown off his hat and held out his arms, but she'd hesitated.

"Where's Lionel?"

The Greek man had shaken his head. "I do not know, Julie. We were losing so bad that I came back. We have been defeated. No silver."

"At least you're still in one piece," Julie had said, and giggled as Phillipas swept her from the floor. The sharp stench of gunpowder intoxicated her. She had found herself unable to resist his exploring mouth, his battle-induced lust.

In spite of the danger of Lionel Kemp walking in, they'd made love again and again until exhaustion quieted the fire of their loins. They'd fallen asleep while their bodies were still joined.

Now, as she blinked and studied the rippling curtain that blocked out the world, Julie Golden sighed and ran her fingers through the curly black hairs that festooned Phillapas' chest. She slowly realized something: Lionel hadn't come back.

He couldn't have. Whether it was in victory or defeat, Lionel wouldn't respect their privacy. He would have barged in to gloat if he'd gotten the silver. If not, he would have punished them both.

Could he be—

A warm hand clasped her breasts. Julie's general grunted in his sleep.

Lionel Kemp was dead. The thought seemed to brighten the room. She bent and kissed the man's mouth.

He quickly woke, grabbed her ears and returned the sloppy kiss. It was long and thrashing, but Julie didn't give in to the surge of heat that spread through her body. She broke it.

"Phillipas, Lionel didn't come back last night."

"So?" he pecked her chin.

"Do you think he was killed?"

He sighed and nodded. "Most probably. They knew we were coming, Julie. Magnus knew.

Somehow, they had prepared. We must have lost half our men. I came back to you as soon as I saw that we had no chance of winning. It was no good."

She nodded.

Phillipas sat up. "You are not upset?"

"Not really. Lionel Kemp—" Julie bit her tongue.

The Greek laughed. "I know all about him, what he did to you."

She stared disbelievingly at him.

"He told me on the way to the mine last night. Kemp said that after we had the silver, he would leave Oreville, so it did not matter. He boasted of how he had that young man murdered and tricked you into believing you had done it. He was not good, Julie."

She flushed at the revelation. She knew she hadn't done it! "But you are, Phillipas. You're a very good man!"

"Let us make love again."

Julie sat beside him. "No. Phillipas, we have to get out of here."

"Now?"

"Yes. Now! Get dressed, dear. We're leaving!" She sprang from the bed and tore through her closet.

"But Julie, there are no stagecoaches . . ."

"We'll ride. I haven't been riding for years, but I have done it before." She smiled as she struggled into her bodice. "Don't you see? If they even suspect we were involved they'll come after us."

He grimly nodded. "Okay, Julie. Okay!"

"I have money, Phillipas. When I thought—I mean, just before the attack I drew out my savings. Over $2,000. Lionel would have spent it if he'd known about it, but I never let him know. We can get to some other town and leave all this behind us."

"Yes."

The immigrant stood and collected his clothing from the floor.

"You know, Phillipas? Everything will turn out fine!"

Spur asked at the saloon, but the wary barkeep said that Ma hadn't been in that morning yet—even though it was nine-thirty. Frustrated, he asked Pete to tell him where the woman lived.

"Nothing doing!" he barked. "If you want a girl, I'm the man to see. Tell me which one." Pete blushed, reached under the bar and banged a glass of feathers onto its polished surface. "Well? Which one gets you hard?"

"Never mind."

As he walked to the door he heard glass shatter behind him.

"I ain't doing it no more!" Pete yelled. "I just plumb ain't! Not seemly for a man! No, sir!"

Spur inquired of a well dressed man, who pointed out Julie Golden's house—a large structure on the outskirts of town.

The front door was open. He walked in and checked every room. The place was empty. The stove was cold. The kerosene lamps blazed away in the morning light. There was no sign of Julie Golden.

Back outside, Spur saw fresh hoof prints leading from the house.

If she'd left town she was a smart woman, Spur thought. True, it seemed that everything she'd done had been controlled and instigated by Lionel Kemp, but that would be hard to prove now that he was dead.

At any rate, the silver robberies wouldn't continue.

He closed the door, sighed and walked to Mayor Kincaid's house.

"You have to think about your future, young woman!" Emma Grieve crossed her bony arms. "Only a rich man will give you all the things that this cruel world will stubbornly refuse to hand you on a silver platter. Until you meet the right one you'll have to earn your living. We'll simply have to find you a good position somewhere."

"Really, grandmother!" Melissa smoothed her skirt over her legs as they sat on the porch bench in front of the Eastern Heights Hotel. "Just because you did it, doesn't mean that I have to!"

The elderly woman shook her head. "Did what?"

"You know very well, you old biddy! What Ma made me do!" Melissa's cheeks colored.

Emma Grieve held her breath and chuckled. "Melissa, your mind's a train that always pulls into the same station. Young lady, I'm not talking about that. I can tell it doesn't suit you. But what about the stage?"

Melissa looked away from her. "It doesn't leave until next week."

"Child, listen to me! You have a fine voice. You can dance. Why don't you become an entertainer? You could tour the west, giving shows in saloons, earning good money. The men in lots of these towns are starving for something to look at, to listen to, to dream about. Oh, I know what they say back east about female entertainers. They call them tramps. That may be, but singing and dancing's a might easier to do than earning a living on your back."

Melissa grabbed her grandmother's arm and shushed her. A man in a clerical collar stopped in shock before the women, blanched and hurried off.

"I know," the girl said. "Maybe you're right. It might be fun, dressing up and putting on shows like I used to do every Christmas." She rubbed her palms together.

"You think about it, girl." Emma patted her shoulder. "You could be a big star someday, even go back East, open your own place and settle down there—with or without a fat, rich husband."

Melissa smiled.

"I'm sorry, Mr. McCoy. My father's out doing something or other." Kelly Kincaid licked her lips as she stood in the doorway. "But he thought you might be stopping by, so he left you this note. Please come in."

Spur walked in and took the piece of paper.

"McCoy, stay put until I get back. I'm sure my daughter can entertain you.

                              Kincaid."

He looked up at Kelly. The eighteen year old girl stepped past him and closed the door. She turned her eyes to his and simply stared.

After a heated visual exchange, Kelly smiled. "Will you accept my father's hospitality, Mr. McCoy?"

"Ah, sure! I wouldn't want to offend him." The tension between the man and the young woman grew. It was stifling hot. "After all, he was a great help last night."

"I'm sure he was." Kelly rubbed her thighs. "Well! Let's not waste any time. My father told me to take good care of you."

He chuckled. "You don't mean—"

"That's precisely what I mean, Spur McCoy. And I always obey my father."

McCoy put out his arms. "So start entertaining!"

CHAPTER SIXTEEN

She was young, willing and beautiful. But this wasn't the right time, not here in her father's house. The girl's overture was so explicit that Spur cautiously backed from her.

"You don't mean that. Your father would never consent to you and me—"

"You read the letter to you," Kelly Kincaid pointed out. She ripped the mayor's note from Spur's hand. "Please! I really need it! Besides, my father's no ungrateful idiot. He wanted to thank you for all you've done for him, and I suggested something like this."

"Thank me? *You* suggested this?"

"Yes." She advanced on him like a panther after her prey. Kelly licked her lips and tossed her blonde hair.

Spur thought it over for two seconds, slipped off his coat and unbuttoned his shirt.

"What the hell!"

Kelly giggled, her blue eyes flashing. "You know I can be very *entertaining*. Last time was just a rehearsal for the performance I'm about to give you."

"This is going to get you into trouble some day, young lady!"

She struggled out of her green silk dress. "I keep hoping, Spur. But let's not think about that now."

Spur yanked off his boots and socks, straightened and shoved down his trousers, marvelling at the ferocity of the girl's undressing. She tore at her chemise until it split in half and ripped at the three petticoats that hid the lower half of her delicious anatomy.

"Kelly Kincaid! You'd think you've been without a man for years!"

"Heck, Spur." She smiled as she finally unbuttoned the first petticoat. "A few days is like a year."

She was just as beautiful as he'd remembered, McCoy thought as the woman removed the last two petticoats and stood naked before him. Her skin was as white as eggshell, her hips and breasts curved out in all the right directions. Her body was far more developed and mature than those of many other eighteen year old girls. He reached for her.

"Nothing doing," Kelly said, backing from him until she leaned her nude form against the stair railing. "Get outta your drawers! I wanna see him!"

"Hope you want to do more than see him." Spur smirked and kicked off his underwear. His manhood sprung up between his legs, throbbing and ready for work.

"Yes. Oh, yes!"

Kelly jiggled her shoulders back and forth, pressing her lips together and sat on the third step of the stairs. "Come here, you gorgeous hunk of man!"

Spur forgot the dangerous position the girl had put him in and walked to her. "Kelly, I—"

"Shut up. Don't talk. Just put it in my mouth." She licked her lips.

"What the hell."

Her pretty head was just at the right level. Spur sighed as his toes hit the bottom step. Kelly grabbed his hips and impaled herself on his erection. He gasped at the warm liquidity of her mouth, at the fury of her licking tongue, at the girl's willingness to do this to him.

"Mmmmm."

He fell forward, gripped the newel post and slammed a hand against the wall as she pumped her head between his legs. Spur shivered. His penis slid in and out of her mouth. She was so good, he thought. His body tightened. McCoy stifled a gasp. She was almost too good. His elbows buckled.

"Ah, Kelly!" He regained his balance and lightly gripped her head, guiding her erotic movements, gently thrusting into her accommodating mouth. The silky sensations fanned the heat that pulsed in his body.

She should be choking by now, Spur thought. But she wasn't. She wanted more, more. He slid down her throat.

"Jesus, Kelly!" McCoy snapped out of it. "Come on, little girl. We have to stop. Your father could walk in that door and see us!"

She groaned and took him until his testicles pooled on her cute chin.

"Shit! Kelly, you're too damned good. I'm ready to shoot off in your mouth!"

Kelly still wouldn't stop, so Spur forcibly pulled out of her and stood back. He gasped as his penis spasmed and throbbed, staring in disbelief at the seemingly innocent but gloriously naked young woman.

"Just when it was getting so fine." She pouted and delicately wiped her lips.

"Look, Kelly. Maybe we better go upstairs. To your bedroom. You know? Most people do it in beds."

"Really?"

"Kelly!"

"Ah, don't spoil my fun!"

The lithe young woman spun around, planted her hands on the third step and stuck her beautiful bottom into the air. "Whatever you say, Spur. Let's go right up."

He grunted, appreciating Kelly's round backside. His control broke.

"Come on! Climb onto my back and we'll go to my bedroom. If that's what you really want." Her voice was sexy-husky. "Do you, Spur?"

He laughed. "Okay, little lady. You win." He rubbed his organ against her wet lips. The warmth of her body enflamed him. "You win the grand prize."

"And it sure is grand! Stick it in, Spur! Slam me with your sausage!"

Rubbing her cheeks, he sheathed himself, pushing into her slick opening, unable to stop until he'd drilled as far as he could go. The incredible tight wetness shocked him. Kelly groaned and came alive, bucking, writhing, as raw sensation exploded in her body.

"Yes. Oh, yes!"

Spur reared back and smoothly plowed into her. They were perfect for each other—two people needing the same thing, the same hot pleasures that woman and man have shared since the beginning of time.

Her buttocks bounced as he pumped in and out, slamming himself full-length, enjoying her body. Kelly groaned and flung her head back in time with each of the man's deep, penetrating thrusts.

Spur broke out in sweat. The room heated with the sun and the intensity of their actions. Kelly turned a lust-crazed face toward him and gasped.

"Ram me!"

She worked his penis with her internal muscles. He rode her so hard that his plunging set off her pleasure. The young woman spasmed and screamed as pure electricity exploded through her body. She shook like a wet dog and howled.

As she rocked through her orgasm Spur hunched over her, slapping his hairy chest to her back. He took her hanging breasts in his hands and squeezed her nipples, intensifying the young woman's experience. Feeling those luscious orbs sent him over the edge.

Somewhere far behind him the door opened, but Spur forgot it. His body jerked. Every muscle in his lean frame tightened as he poured his seed into Kelly, blasting his lust into the lovely lady, cursing and gasping and hugging her as he shook through his ultimate pleasure.

It was too soon but he didn't care. Spur ecstatically roared. He slowed his spastic pumps, edging away from the moment until they were firmly connected and their drenched bodies were plastered together.

"Ah, um, I'll leave you two alone."

Dazed from the sex, Spur turned a weary head behind him. Mayor Justin Kincaid shot him a funny smile.

"May—Kin—I mean!" One last tremor rippled through him. "I can—"

He laughed. "McCoy, you better get some rest. Looks like you need it." Justin Kincaid left his house.

"Kelly, ah, Kelly!" McCoy said. He started to pull out of her but the woman slammed back against his thighs.

"What?"

"Your father—"

"Don't—don't worry about him." She gasped and pleasurably groaned. "I told you. He's used to seeing me like this. Besides, he said I could."

Spur nodded, though she couldn't see it. The young woman slowly lifted her body onto the third step. McCoy moved with her, maintaining their pulsating contact until he was curled up behind her. They lay on the cool wood until their heartbeats levelled and their breathing returned to normal.

"Your father's almost as remarkable as you," he said.

"Thanks!" Kelly sighed and twisted her head around. "Spur McCoy, that was absolutely exhausting." She quickly pressed her full lips to his.

THE MINER'S MOLL

165

"Agreed," he said, kissing the girl's nose.
"And I think we should do it again."
He groaned.

Two hours after he'd first walked into Justin
Kincaid's house, Spur let the mayor's daughter
bathe him. He dressed and finally managed to leave
the still unsatisfied girl.

A woman like that could be dangerous to a man,
he thought as he walked to the telegraph office. In
more ways than one.

McCoy sent a telegram to General Halleck. In it
he detailed the things he'd accomplished in Oreville.
The robberies were permanently stopped. He'd
prevented the success of a major attack against
Cleve Magnus's mine. The one man responsible was
unavoidably dead. Spur said that he was ready for
his next assignment.

He had no qualms about letting Cleve Magnus kill
Lionel Kemp early that morning. It may not have
been right, but Spur couldn't have stopped it.
Besides, in the miner's mind, the battle that had
raged last night was still going on.

As he walked from the telegraph office into the
blazing desert sunshine, Spur reseated his newly
bought hat (to replace the one he'd lost track of
during his swim in the Merrone River) and headed
for the Eastern Heights Hotel.

Three days until the next stage out of town. He
could buy a horse and leave, but he deserved a short
holiday. It would give him time to ride out to see
Magnus again.

The man saved him a trip out to the mine. Cleve
rode up to the hotel and dismounted just as Spur

was walking in.

"McCoy! Just wanted to thank you," the short miner said as he tied up his horse at the hitching post.

Spur smiled. "No thanks necessary. You know that I was just doing my job."

"Yeah, sure. Lots of men could have ridden into my camp and saved my butt the way you did!" He snorted. "You know exactly what you were guarding? You want to know how much smelted silver I had in the house?"

"Tell me."

"I just finished counting it before I rode into town. Five-thousand pounds."

Spur whistled. "I guess there'll be no problem in you supplying the Bureau of Engraving and Printing with the silver they need."

"Nope."

"How many men did you lose?"

Magnus grabbed his hat. "Too many. Twenty. I'll never be able to repay the bastard who had them killed."

"You, ah, already did." Spur looked up at the sky and whistled.

"Come on, McCoy! Kincaid told me that he was already dead when I shot him out there!"

"I lied. To get you off the hook. Hope it lets you get some sleep at night." He slapped the miner's shoulder and laughed. "Phineas."

The miner's face reddened. "So? Yeah? What's your first name, McCoy? You didn't get that moniker while you was a little sucking baby! They didn't call you Spur then!"

He turned and walked into the hotel. "True," he

said, "but they sure as hell didn't call me Phineas!"

Twenty miles from Oreville, Julie Golden broke twigs between her hands and made kindling. Phillipas dumped an armload of wood in front of her.

He produced some matches, expertly laid the wood and touched a flaming lucifer to the stack. The fire crackled into life. Phillipas drove a forked stick into the ground beside it and hooked on the coffee pot.

At midday, the sun burned directly overhead. The heat from the fire made Julie move away from it. A bird twittered as it flew overhead.

"You ever get used to those stupid saddles? I'm rubbed raw down there!" she said, soothing the inside of her thighs.

The Greek laughed. "Yes, in time."

"I'll believe you because it's less painful than the alternative." She fixed her green eyes on his. "Where should we go?"

He shrugged. "I do not know. You're the boss."

"Stop saying that, Phillipas!" Julie tossed her head and stood. The pain intensified. "Hell, if I had my way we'd stay here. I never want to see another horse again!"

Her mount whinneyed.

"I think that would be fine with her."

"You—you!"

Julie fell onto him, knocking the sturdy man to the sand. She chewed on his moustache and peppered his face with kisses.

"Julie, my Julie."

Satisfied at her revenge, she slipped to the ground

and nuzzled his neck. "You know who told Magnus about us? About our attack?"

"No," he said, biting her ear.

"Ouch! Whoever it was, I guess I owe him a favor." She sighed at the feeling of Phillipas' tongue and teeth.

"Why? He ruined everything! We didn't get one ounce of silver!"

"Quite true, my Greek friend. But I got the best thing of all. You."

He laughed and kicked the coffeepot onto the fire. Phillipas pushed Julie onto the dirt as the flames sputtered and went out.